Winter Horrorland

Undertaker Books

UNDERTAKER BOOKS

www.undertakerbooks.com

Contents

D.L.'s Bit...

Ugh. So much to do, and Cyan's breathing down my neck for the introduction for *Winter Horrorland*. There just aren't enough hours in the day...

Wait. I've got a co-editor on this one. I'll make *them* do the introduction!

Yes, this should work nicely... He's done such a good job with everything else, doing the introduction won't be an issue. Besides, it's not like anyone reads them.

Oh, Avery...

-D.L. Winchester
Newport, TN
12/1/2024

Introduction From Avery Lewis

Thanks, D.L. Let me just set aside this ten-page essay...

When I started my internship at Undertaker Books, I wasn't much of a horror writer. I like horror movies and writing, but I liked them separately before now. I'm honestly not even sure why.

After a particularly engaging hour and twenty minutes with Rebecca, I stumbled across this internship one day. I took an Intro to Creative Writing course with her during my second semester as a transfer student, and I loved her energy. Naturally, I registered for another course with her. Now, I don't just say nice things about her because I work under her, and because she grades my stories. (Maybe a little.) She warned me that she would indoctrinate me into horror, and I'm damn glad she did. This internship as a whole and working on this anthology have been fantastic learning opportunities. From helping choose the pieces to editing them, I've had a lot of firsts with these bewitching stories bound in ice-cold dread.

Growing up in Upstate New York, snow is no stranger to me. The fright it can create isn't, either. Being home alone around the holidays or fearing your snowmen might awaken one night—just a few I resonated with. I'm not scared of snowmen anymore, though. Just when I was a kid. Totally.

Oh, there's an email from Rebecca right now. I should finish this before I have to trek through three feet of snow to her class...

D.L. and I have curated these ten chilling, wintery tales. They may seem unassuming at first, like the start of a blizzard, but each word adds to the terror before they inevitably bury you in it. From zen retreats out in the winter woods to ancient horrors that slumber beneath the snow, there's bound to be a story or two that will make your blood run cold.

These stories prove that even the warmest hearth can't keep the darkness from pulling you into its icy grip. So crank up your heat, settle in with a mug of hot chocolate, and prepare to feel the chill creep in. We hope you enjoy your venture into *Winter Horrorland.*

-**Avery Lewis**
Fredonia, NY
12/4/2024

.

SWEET ELSIE

CASSANDRA DAUCUS

T he wind howled outside the farmhouse, rattling the windowpanes and sending shivers down Elsie's spine. The flames danced and flickered, casting long shadows across the otherwise dark bedroom. Elsie, seated in a chair by the fireplace, wrapped her woolen shawl tighter around her shoulders, trying to ward off the chill that seemed to seep into her bones despite the warmth of the fire.

Papa stood silent behind her, his weathered hands deftly weaving her hair.

"Wish we had a looking glass." Elsie gazed into the fire as she spoke.

Papa pulled the ribbon tight around the end of her braid. "God don't care how you look, so you shouldn't care either." His voice carried the weariness of a man who had seen much hardship in his lifetime and didn't expect things to change.

Elsie sighed and toyed with the lace cuffs of her nightgown. She would simply admire herself in the tintype hung on the wall instead. It was a few years old, from when Elsie was just sixteen and Peter was twelve. Although Papa aged since it had been taken, he insisted she still looked the same, with golden hair and lovely blue eyes and a figure as fetching as anyone's. But as Elsie studied the faded image, she couldn't help but feel a pang in her chest.

Elsie had hit her head when she fell off a cliff back in the autumn. The bump had knocked all her memories right out of her head, and she'd been left with headaches that made her see stars, which would come and go whenever they pleased. She wished, more than anything, that she could remember her childhood.

Elsie's reverie was interrupted by a knock on the front door of their farmhouse. Papa's hands found her shoulders; at the pressure, she drew in a breath and held it. They waited. There was another knock. This time it was accompanied by a shout.

"Hello!" The shout was quickly followed by another thump against the door. "Please, open the door! It's cold! Please! I'm looking for someone!"

Elsie's heart raced as she turned to look at Papa. The winter storm raged outside, and the thought of someone out in the wind and snow sent a shiver down her spine. But the wrinkle between Papa's eyes deepened with distrust.

"Must be crazy to be out in the snow at night like this," he growled. "Don't want no crazy man in my house, especially not with you still hurtin' after your fall."

Elsie bit her lip, torn between sympathy for the stranger and her father's caution.

At that moment, a burst of wind jostled the house, howling like an angry beast, and the urgency of the situation tugged at her heart.

"But it's so cold."

Snow had been falling all day and the previous night, heavy and wet. Elsie wasn't allowed near the windows, on account of the drafts, but she'd seen it on Papa when he'd come in from attending to his chores. He'd go out dry and come back soaked, his salt-and-golden curls dusted with white that turned to thick drops in a matter of seconds.

"Please, Papa," she whispered, and set her face the way she'd learned would soften him. "Let the man in. It is awful cold out there."

"No," he replied. "Stay quiet. He'll go."

But the visitor didn't go; he knocked and yelled for minutes, crying out about how he just wanted to talk to them, to ask if they'd seen someone he was trying to find. Meanwhile, Elsie and Papa waited in silence.

"Papa," she whispered, frustrated with both her father and the stranger at the door. "He knows we're here. Just go down and see what he wants."

Papa hesitated, his gaze softening slightly as he regarded his daughter. Finally, with a resigned sigh, he nodded. "Very well," he conceded, his voice gruff but with a hint of compassion. "I'll go down and let him sit a spell before I send him away."

"Thank you, Papa."

He grunted, unsmiling, then offered her his hand. "Do you want me to help you to bed before I go?"

"I'm fine," Elsie said, reaching for the thing that always gave her comfort—the leather-bound family Bible that sat on the table by her elbow. "You can help me to bed once he's gone."

The fall haunted her like a ghost she couldn't quite see, but the mess in her head was only half of it. She'd also broken her ankle. Despite Papa's best efforts to tend to her injury, the bone healed crookedly, leaving her with a pronounced limp that made every step a painful reminder of her own frailty.

5

But Elsie refused to be confined to her bed like a fragile porcelain doll. When Papa was out attending to his chores with the farmhands he kept at a distance from their home, she would seize the opportunity to venture out of bed, her determination outweighing the pain that gnawed at her every step. Elsie would hobble around her room with a stubbornness that she thought might make her papa proud, if he ever found out about it—although she dreaded the punishment that would come if he did discover her secret. She would trace the contours of the furniture as she navigated her way with cautious determination, hoping that in time the feeling of the wood under her fingertips would become familiar.

When she grew restless, Elsie would venture farther, her trembling fingers grasping the smooth wooden banister as she made her way down the narrow staircase that led to the lower level of their home. Each step was a testament to her resilience, a silent defiance against the confines of her own body and the suffocating attention of her doting father.

Papa insisted on hovering over her like a protective shadow, his presence a constant reminder of her vulnerability. He would fuss and fret over her every move, his worry etched deep into the lines of his face as he tended to her every need with a fervent devotion that bordered on stifling.

And while Elsie was grateful for his care, his well-meaning gestures served only to remind her of the life she had lost but couldn't remember, and the uncertainty that lay ahead. At the same time, Elsie knew that Papa's love was the only anchor tethering her to the world she once knew, a fragile lifeline in a sea of uncertainty and despair.

Another knock echoed through the house, and Papa took three long strides to the bedroom door. He opened it before glancing back at her, face grave.

"You," he pointed one long, strong finger at her, "you keep quiet, Elsie. I don't want any man knowing you're here. Do you understand me?"

"Yes, Papa," Elsie replied. "I understand." She didn't, not really, but Papa didn't need to know that.

"Good girl. Read your scripture, and I'll be back up to say goodnight once he's gone."

He disappeared into the hallway, closing the door behind him. Heavy footfalls thumped down the stairs, and moments later she could hear the shuffle of feet and the murmur of voices in the kitchen below.

Elsie tried to read, but she was unable to find purchase in the words of Paul. Instead, she flipped to the back of the book, where her family generations were listed down the page, each one added as they were born along with dates of marriage and death. There were Papa's grandparents, his papa and mama, and then Papa himself and Mama, too. Finally, there was Elsie, her brother Peter, and another girl called Grace who had died before Elsie was born. Elsie traced her brother's name. Poor Peter: he'd been only fourteen when he and mother had fallen ill and died back in the summer. His bed still lurked in the opposite corner of the room, cold and empty. Elsie hated that she couldn't remember him; she was sure that she'd loved him more than anything. Felt it in her bones.

She touched her own name and her date of birth. Beside that, in place of a death date, there was a strange rough patch, as though something had scraped across the paper but not quite hard enough to tear. Elsie's brow furrowed as she rubbed her finger over the patch. But try as she might, the memories remained elusive, slipping through her mind like dried kernels of maize through her fingers. She closed her eyes, willing herself to remember, to grasp hold of even the faintest whisper of her past. But it was no use. The void that had consumed her memories remained as vast and impenetrable as ever, leaving her with nothing but questions and a sense of profound loss.

"I ain't seen no woman." Papa's voice rumbled up from the kitchen, punctuated by a gust of wind that whistled through the eaves.

Elsie set down the Bible. The stranger was looking for a woman. The notion tugged on her heart, and she wasn't certain why. Perhaps it was because her own mother was gone—dead, of course, not missing—and it was only natural that she would feel for someone else who had also lost someone.

The stranger responded, but his voice was too quiet for Elsie to hear. Papa always said that curiosity wasn't befitting a well-bred young woman, but Elsie didn't care. She raised herself out of her chair and, as quietly as she could while being careful of her bad ankle, lowered herself to the ground. The quiet hum of conversation in the kitchen never paused.

Elsie scooted across the rag rug to the hardwood as quietly as possible. There were spaces between some of the boards, and she found a spot where she could both see and hear the stranger below.

"... my mother. Since October. Are you sure you haven't seen her?"

There was a pen-and-ink drawing laid on the table between the two men, which stared up at the ceiling where Elsie stared down. It was a portrait of a sturdy-looking middle-aged woman, with dark hair and eyes, and a serious countenance. As for the stranger, Elsie could see no more than the top of his head, which was covered with long, dark hair, pulled low into a ponytail. He wore a jacket of brown wool, very wet and worn and not nearly warm enough for the weather. Elsie found herself drawn to the stranger, almost as though she knew him. She thought he reminded her of Peter. She wanted to see his face. Slowly, carefully, she crawled across the floor and opened the bedroom door. The doorknob usually rattled, but she had learned how to hold it to keep it quiet.

She made her way out onto the landing. From there, all she had to do was put her hands down two steps...maybe three...and then she could lean down. The kitchen was right there. She could lean...just a peek.

With a shriek, Elsie tumbled down the stairs. Miraculously, although it was a fright, all the fall did was knock the air out of her. But she was so surprised she didn't perceive the cacophony in the kitchen until somebody grabbed her.

"Mother!" The face of the stranger filled her vision. He was younger than she had expected, not much more than a boy—*Peter*, her mind insisted—with a round face and keen brown eyes. His smile blinded her. "Mother! You're alive. Alive!"

Elsie couldn't make sense of his words, and still they hit her like a punch. *Mother*. She stared into the young man's face, explored his eyes, searched the lines of his brow and nose and jaw for anything familiar. Was there something? Or was her suggestive mind playing tricks? Overwhelmed, she snapped her head toward Papa, but he was glaring at the stranger with an expression of equal parts fear and longing.

"Peter." Papa's voice was as tight as his hands, clenched at his sides. "You could be Peter. Have you come back to be with me and my Elsie?"

"Who is Peter?" the stranger asked, tugging on Elsie's arms, encouraging her to stand. "I'm not Peter. I'm here for my mother."

"Papa?" Elsie asked. She was so confused. Why was he yelling about Peter? And the stranger's exclamation kept ringing in her ears, unsettling her even further. He called her *mother*. "Papa, what–"

Papa interrupted her question with a scream and a crash. He had overturned the kitchen table and swung at it with the heavy iron poker from the cast iron stove. The dark-haired woman's portrait fluttered into a puddle left by the stranger's boots. Papa pointed the poker at them, his voice hard and dripping with vinegar.

"You may not want to be Peter, but she is my daughter. My *daughter*. Sweet Elsie."

The stranger dragged Elsie towards the door, panicked, and Elsie froze in fear and confusion. She didn't know if she should fight to stay with Papa, or fight to go with the stranger.

"What are you talking about?" the stranger yelled. "You're mad. She's nearly as old as you. This woman is my *mother*. Her name is—"

Papa howled and smashed the heavy iron poker into the stranger's skull. Elsie closed her eyes against the brutality, screaming while Papa struck the stranger again and again. She screamed until he stopped, and the world was warm and wet, and smelled of copper.

Mother.

Papa dropped the poker. "I'm sorry you had to see that," he said, calm as you please, as he might apologize for stepping on an ant. "But you and Mama and Peter were already taken from me once, and I'm not about to let that happen again."

Elsie was so full of terror, she feared it would never stop. She had no words for Papa, there was nothing she could say to him. He didn't seem to need a reply. "I'll be back soon and then I'll get you all cleaned up and tucked into bed."

Elsie shuddered as she stared at the bloody bundle curled up on the ground next to her. Her voice shook as she reached out to touch the long brown hairs that stuck to the puddle of gore spread across the floor. "What will you do with him?"

Papa grunted, pulled the stranger out of her grasp, and lifted him up by his shoulders. Crimson streaks showed bold against the wood as he dragged the body toward the door. "I'll put him in the barn. Once the snow lets up—tomorrow, maybe, or the next day—I'll take him into the woods. There's a crack in the earth there..." He paused and eyed her. "Actually, it's not too far from where you fell, Elsie. I'll drop him in there, and nobody will ever find him."

Elsie shivered when Papa opened the door, inviting in a blast of freezing air, and she shivered again after he closed it. The discarded portrait lay across the ruined kitchen. She crawled through the stranger's blood to reach it, and she imagined that every sticky touch of her hand was a caress. The portrait was logged with water, but she could still make out the basic outline of the woman's face.

His mother.

The stranger said Elsie was *her*.

Elsie's memory was as empty and black as the crack in the earth, but she had to know. She no longer trusted Papa, but her reflection in the window wouldn't lie. Drafts be damned. She limped across the room, held her breath, and with a trembling hand she pushed the curtain aside.

Inspired by H. P. Lovecraft, M. R. James, Shirley Jackson, Robert Aickman, and a ton of fan fiction, Cassandra Daucus (she/her)

writes a spectrum of horror. She is intrigued by how the human mind responds to the unknown, and also enjoys a good gross-out. She has stories published and forthcoming in several literary magazines and anthologies, including Not One Of Us and All Existing Literary Magazine. Cassandra lives outside of Philadelphia with her family and two cats. Her social media and website can be found at https://linktr.ee/residualdreaming

THE SNOWMEN

ALEX MCGILVERY

I parked the car outside the gate of the old cemetery, then jumped out and tossed a snowball at Calvin as he got out of the car. He'd dragged me out here to make scary snowmen. Being named after a comic strip character went to his head. I didn't mind; acting young and foolish on occasion help me deal with the world.

The snow after the early spring storm was perfect for making snowmen. It packed nicely yet didn't soak my hands to the bone. I giggled along with him as we put together an army of deformed snow creatures. By the time we were done, the cemetery might have been the site of a new Cambrian explosion with snow things featuring extra limbs and multiple heads. We used branches and busted fence boards for arms. Lacking coal, we used bits of rock and gravel for eyes.

Nobody bothered us; the cemetery had become a no-man's land after the last board member died, along with all the records, in a fire back when we were kids. In the summer, it was filled with blueberries that no one would pick, and now, after a long day of feverish creation, it was filled with monsters.

Calvin laughed maniacally and waved his arms over the cemetery.

"Rise, rise, and take your vengeance on this twisted world."

I tossed another snowball at him, nailing the side of his head. Immediately, the war was on. We sniped at each other as we wove through the snow things, ducking for cover, all while screaming with laughter.

Trying to throw a snowball, then roll behind a monster, I crashed into the thing and knocked it over. Calvin frowned at me.

"It's just a snowman." I rolled off the remains.

"I worked extra hard on that one." He put his hands on his hips. "Now you've gone and wrecked it."

"Sorry." I stood up and stretched. "Let's head home for a hot toddy. I'm beat."

"Fine." He turned and stomped away toward the car.

I sighed and glanced back at the fallen monster. Calvin's moods shifted faster than the weather, but it wasn't like he'd chosen to be that way. ADHD wasn't easy to live with, whether it messed with your wiring or your lover's. Trudging back to the car, I slid into the seat and drove us home along the winding road through the forest that surrounded the cemetery.

Calvin woke early and had coffee on while he made waffles. I gave him a kiss before setting the table, putting the syrup and whipped cream out, and thawing berries. We stuffed ourselves in silence.

"Sorry, I didn't mean to get pouty on you yesterday." Calvin put his fork down and reached over to take my hand.

"Apology accepted. I have a bit of work to do today." I gave him a squeeze and stood up. "Do you want help with the dishes?"

"No, doing dishes is good for me, I like the progression from chaos to order."

"And here I am heading out to bring chaos to the order of my studio."

"Have fun." Calvin laughed and shooed me off.

Studio was a fancy name for a corner of the basement of our tiny house. I cut off a slab of clay and wrapped up the rest again. I'd built a table from two-by-fours so it would be sturdy enough as I wedged the clay to get rid of all the air bubbles. The process of slamming the clay into the table over and over allowed me to express my frustrations in a useful way. I imagined the bubbles to be my resentment and hurt feelings. The violence excised them.

Movies and books insisted that once you'd had that first kiss, everything would be deliriously good.

They lied.

I had my ways of dealing with the disappointment of that lie. Calvin's methods involved waffle batter and dirty dishes.

The wheel in the corner called to me. After wrapping most of the wedged clay in another damp cloth, I sat down, ready to do battle. Potters talked about throwing pots as a kind of zen where they lost themselves in the process. Not me, I had to work the clay, battling my impatience on one hand and perfectionism on the other.

The pot twisted into something ugly, and I smashed it down to start over. Again, it twisted in my hands, but as I moved to destroy it, the image of Calvin's face when I knocked over his snow monster flashed into my mind. It wasn't the pot's fault. I cut it from the wheel and set it on the table. If ugly was the order of the day, then I'd go full-on.

Calvin came down the stairs and interrupted the addition of another tentacle to pothulhu.

"I love it." His eyes gleamed as he ran a finger along the clay. "I'm going out to the cemetery to check on our snow monsters."

"Give me a minute to wash up, and I'll come with you." I moved the thing to the drying shelf, then scrubbed the clay from my hands and arms, hanging my apron on its hook.

"I wanted to see what they look like after the snow." Calvin drove our little car expertly through the new snow, then spoiled his responsible driving by turning donuts in the little parking lot. I whooped along with him. Nothing wrong with a little harmless recklessness.

We climbed from the car and leaned on the fender to admire the circles he'd drawn. Once the adrenaline subsided, we turned to the cemetery. Where I'd expected to see snow-covered monstrosities, there was nothing. Not even bumps in the snow marked where the creatures we'd worked so hard to create had been.

"Looks like they walked away." Calvin stomped through the snow to stand in the middle of the graves.

"Don't say such creepy things." I wrapped my arms around myself to dispel the chill. "Snow men can't walk."

"You're right." He bent to scoop up a handful of snow. "Not the right stuff for snowmen today. Let's go home." The car lights flashed as he unlocked the doors.

As we headed back to the car, something shambled out of the woods to block our path. It lurched on uneven legs and carried a spare head in its third arm. The gravel had slipped to give it a definite leer.

"What is that?" I clutched Calvin's arm.

"It's the snow monster you knocked over." Calvin tilted his head. "I didn't expect them to actually listen to me."

"Tell it to stop." My teeth chattered, and not from the cold. I couldn't believe Calvin wasn't freaking out.

"Stop." Calvin held his hand out like a cop stopping a car. The monster ignored him, reaching out with its two empty arms.

"You go left, and I'll go right." Calvin gave me a gentle push. "It's slower than we are."

I took off like the scared rabbit I was and made it to the car. The snowmonster's extra head slammed into the door as I dove into the seat.

Calvin slid into the driver's seat, started the car, and goosed it into a spin. The back end of the car smashed into the snow monster. I winced at the thought of the fender crumpling as I buckled my seatbelt. Calvin headed away down the road at high speed. Other snow monsters trudged out of the forest to block the way.

"I didn't think we'd built that many." I clutched at the door as we plowed through one after another.

"We didn't." Calvin slalomed the car through three monsters, leaving them as piles of snow. "They must have made more."

The road grew thick with monsters, and our little car couldn't handle their numbers. Calvin missed a corner and crashed into the forest. The airbags exploded and punched me in the face.

I woke in darkness. Calvin's seat was empty, and the door hung open. My door was crumpled against a tree, forcing me to crawl across the seat to escape. Swiveling my head to check for monsters made it grate painfully.

The light from my cell lit the road as I slogged toward home. All the way through the woods, I jumped at every noise, expecting a monster to leap out at me. Between the moments of terror, I worried about Calvin. He'd never have left me alone in the car.

I reached the end of the cemetery road and looked out on the welcoming lights of our neighborhood. The streets were plowed but empty, but that only made it easier to run home. Then I got close enough to hear the screams. Snow monsters wandered through the neighbourhood; the blood-chilling sounds came from them. As we'd found at the cemetery parking lot, they were slow, but they teamed up to block my path. I had to dodge around, careful not to let too many get between me and my goal, slowing my progress until a stitch in my side made me only barely faster than them.

A monster stood on the walk to our front door. I faked going left, then staggered right.

"Don't leave me." Calvin's voice came from the monster. I couldn't help but stop and stare at it. Even in the dark, I could see the black blotches that had to be his blood. He had one arm made of a splintered two-by-four, another of a branch with four fingers. As he slumped toward me, I stumbled back, tripping on the steps, then crawled to the door and fumbled with the key.

I slammed the door shut just as Calvin reached for me, then wailed. It would have been better if I'd died in the car. Part of me sneered that, of course, I focused on my pain, not the destruction of the world.

"Don't cry." Calvin's voice came through the door. "It's all my fault; you're better off without me."

"Don't talk like that." I leaned against the door, too afraid to open it, too afraid to run away from it. "I can't live without you."

Calvin banged on the door. "Come with me."

"I can't." I thought of pothulhu with the tentacles that made him smile and covered my eyes. "I'm afraid."

"Come." Calvin's voice shifted, becoming deeper, rougher.

"No." Pain shot through my heart at rejecting him. I looked down and saw his two-by-four arm sticking out of my chest. Twiggy fingers gripped the door and tore it from its hinges. He dragged me back into the night. I didn't have the breath to scream as he dropped me into the snow on the front lawn.

"Join us." Calvin pushed snow over me. The cold eased my pain until I stood up beside my love.

"Let's go build more snowmen."

Alex McGilvery has been reading since before he can remember, and writing almost that long. He has published more than 35 books and is author and editor at his imprint Celticfrog Publishing. Alex lives in Clearwater with his dog and the stories clawing their way out of his head.

THE IVORIES

MORGAN CHALFANT

Piano music trickled over the bar interior like the piano woman's fingers trickled over her ivory keys. Her long, white-polished fingers danced over the ivories in a blur of purity and passion for her art. Her movements were sharp and aggressive as the crescendo came, then sensual and flowing as the music slowed down. It was like she was touching a lover. From a plush black lounge chair in the far corner, Trevor Cunningham watched the piano girl, wishing with reckless abandon that she would play him like she did her piano and allow him to pluck at her own strings.

Her name was Penelope. He knew little about her other than her name, which the over-the-hill bartender had spilled to him for twenty bucks the first night he had wandered into the quaint little piano bar called Longitude. He'd needed a break from working on his graduate degree studies. Trevor had precious few extracurricular activities other than his nightly outings. Since then, he had come to the bar six nights in a row for the great pleasure of witnessing Penelope's talent—and hoping to one day be a part of it.

Trevor knew he should be working on his own music but couldn't pry himself away from his seat. As a graduate student majoring in music education, he could not discount his affinity for the lovely tones coming from Penelope's piano as *part* of the reason he stayed—but the majority of his interest lay with the girl responsible for their creation. Not even the large snowflakes falling outside could stop him from hearing Penelope play. A wintery rush washed across the interior as a patron pushed open the door and left the bar. Trevor felt the frigid draft, but did not take his eyes from the piano and its player.

The snow persisted. And so did Penelope. Tonight, like all nights, she sat on the padded piano bench in a short black dress that clung to her long slender frame, with skin as pure porcelain white as the piano keys she played. Her dark red hair was pulled back into a ponytail. Demure black glasses framed her muted, soft features. Her feet pressed the pedals in unison with her fluttering fingers.

Beethoven's "Moonlight Sonata" was the piece of choice. Trevor sipped his whiskey and listened to her finish the song—rapid strikes on the keys, rolling scales, and a gentle swaying motion of her body. Sometimes, Trevor got so lost in the tones he wasn't sure if she was driving the music or if it was driving her.

Longitude was never that busy. These days, a piano bar only had a niche demographic. A few other customers sat at the bar on the other side of the stage, more engrossed in the muted television broadcasting a football game than in the here and now. A fifty-something woman wearing pearls and a turquoise dress sat at a table with a grey-bearded man who appeared to be her husband. She stood up and made her way toward the restrooms in back, not paying any attention to the piano girl.

Trevor shook his head in dismay and returned his gaze to Penelope as her hands came to a halt and the echo of the music died slowly, ebbing away into the darkness of the room. She closed the lid down over the piano keys, scooted the bench backward and stood up.

As she stepped down from the stage, her eyes turned to meet his. Deep brown orbs framed in glass and plastic. She smiled warmly. Trevor smiled back. Their exchange lasted a mere second, but in that second, Trevor was held captive for what felt like hours. Penelope strode across the bar, disappearing behind a curtain obscuring an **EMPLOYEES ONLY** area.

Trevor checked his watch, already knowing what time it was due to Penelope's prompt exit. Sure enough, eleven o'clock on the dot. His heart thumped momentously in his chest. Though the exchange of smiles was brief, it was the first moment in all his visits that she had acknowledged him as she retired for the night.

He finished his drink while the customers at the bar filed out of the building. The couple at the table left. Trevor grabbed his coat. Instead of leaving his glass on the table beside his chair, he walked over to the bar and set it on the counter within reach of the bartender.

"Thank you," the bartender said in a gravelly voice.

The man's posture was hunched, and he had a small but noticeable limp. His hair was turning white at the temples. The tangibility of stress was evident in his features. Pockmarks rimmed his nose and the crow's feet at the corners of his eyes indicated a life of menial labor.

"Looks like you're the last man standing," the bartender said, clearing his throat.

"Looks like it." Trevor flipped open his wallet and passed the man a twenty-dollar bill. "Keep it all. Tell Penelope her music was transcendent as usual."

"Transwhat?" He shot Trevor a confused look. "Hold on a sec, you can tell her yourself." He swept the bar rag over his shoulder, leaned through the black curtain behind him, and barked, "Penelope! Come out here, will you?"

Trevor was about to protest but stopped himself. It was about time he actually spoke to his nightly muse. *Courage, Trevor. Courage.*

A beautiful white hand swept aside the curtain, contrasting sharply with the black fabric. The moment Penelope stepped through; the bartender smirked. Trevor tried to say hi, but his tongue suddenly felt as silent as a broken piano key.

"Honey, this fella's taken a shine to you tickling the ivories." He leaned across the bar and made a come-hither motion to Trevor with a leathery index finger. "My daughter. Ivories better be the only thing being tickled." He smiled, but Trevor knew what that smile meant. *Hurt my daughter, and I'll find a place to bury you deep.*

Trevor was not deterred. "Yes, sir," he responded politely.

The bartender left them alone, disappearing through the same curtain his daughter had just come through. Penelope smiled at him warmly.

"Don't worry about him," she said. "He's just a lil' protective."

"Can't say I blame him," Trevor replied. "You...you play beautifully."

She covered her mouth with a hand and chuckled. Letting her hand fall away, she said, "Thank you. Judging by your streak of nights sitting over there, I figured at the very least, you didn't hate it."

"Are you kidding?!" he exclaimed. "You're amazing. You're like the white keys on your piano. Shiny and perfect." Trevor had to take a deep breath and rein himself in. "Uh, I mean, you're...you're welcome," he stuttered. He could feel his heart rate rising. This woman was truly special. "Damn, how transparent am I?"

Penelope held up her beautiful fingers. "Just a little bit."

"Would it be totally weird if I asked, can I buy you a drink?"

"I drink for free..." She flashed him a smirk.

"Well, fine then, I'll buy you as many as you want," Trevor said.

He couldn't believe a line that smooth had just left his mouth. Penelope seemed to like it, judging from her laughter. That, or she was laughing at how pathetic his vain attempts at getting to know her were. Trevor's few pursuits had not often ended in success.

"I'm Trevor, by the way," he said, stretching his hand over the bar.

She put her hand in his, and it was the best thing that had happened to him since listening to her music. Her fingertips were calloused, conditioned from repetitively striking keys, but her palms were warm and soft.

"Penelope," she said.

"I know."

"Oh, do you?"

Trevor nodded honestly. "I bribed your father for your name a few nights ago."

"How much did it take?"

"Twenty bucks and an agreement to buy at least two drinks."

Penelope grabbed a damp rag and wiped it across the bar surface, no doubt to help out her father. She did strike Trevor as the dutiful daughter type.

"Speaking of drinks..." Penelope paused. "It's awful cold out. I was just about to make myself some tea upstairs. Like a cup?"

"Yes" left his mouth almost before her question was finished. Only after it left his mouth did he realize how overzealous his tone had been as the word echoed through the empty bar.

Penelope's eyes widened, and her lips spread into the broadest smile Trevor had ever seen. Seeing her smile was a strange and lovely experience. She never smiled when she played the piano. The entire time she worked the ivories, her face was always stone, devoid of emotion, like she was focused on the music, and not a single errant thought could distract her. Now, she was different. Different than he expected. Not as introverted as he assumed. On the contrary, she seemed to love the attention. *His* attention.

"Come on," she said, waving him around the bar.

Penelope led him into the back and up an old wooden staircase that wound around in three separate flights. She opened the door at the top of the stairs and let him enter first, holding the door open for him.

He gave her an appreciative nod and went inside. She followed, closing the door behind them.

It was clear to Trevor from the interior that this was Penelope's loft apartment. In the corner nearest the door was a vintage record player sitting atop an old, wheeled cart. On the bottom shelf of the cart was stacked a pile of record albums. The curtains were lavender with strange black patterns printed on them. A small kitchen existed toward the back with a wooden partition separating the kitchen from the living room. Against one wall was a tiny bookshelf with a row of books filled with all sorts of musical numbers from the greatest composers ever to have lived--Mozart, Chopin, Wagner, Vivaldi, and of course, Beethoven.

Penelope slipped off her black flats and put them by the door. Trevor followed suit, unlacing his sneakers and taking them off. The apartment had old orange and brown shag carpet that looked straight out of the 1970s. Still, it felt soft on the feet.

"Have a seat," she said.

Trevor nodded. "Thanks." He couldn't help but glance at her cute tiny feet as she padded across the floor, white toenails clashing against the brown patches of the carpet. Trevor meandered farther into the apartment, scanning the beige-colored walls with his eyes.

Penelope strolled over to a small electric stove and began boiling water in an old cast iron kettle. Alongside the oven, on the kitchen counter, there were multiple spools of piano wire, pliers, and wire cutters.

"You do your own piano maintenance, too?" Trevor inquired. "I'm impressed."

"Yeah." She nodded, glancing back at him. "I hate the maintenance, but it has to be done...like so many things in life we hate."

"The instrument is only as tuned as its musician," Trevor answered.

"Exactly." She chuckled. "You do understand."

Trevor detected something solemnly unique to her manner. Her eyes brimmed with some measure of melancholy behind the friendly smile and laughter.

Then he caught sight of the decorations hanging on one wall. It was covered in framed pieces of paper. He moved closer so that he could read them. As he closed in, he could see they were all prestigious letters of acceptance to the best musical arts colleges in a number of different countries. Juilliard. The Royal College of Music in the United Kingdom. Vienna, Austria's University of Music and Performing Arts. *Why wasn't Penelope playing at any of them?* He was no expert, but his ear was not entirely untrained from majoring in the music field, and he could say even without seeing the acceptance letters, she was quite good at what she did.

Trevor turned and saw Penelope positioning tea bags in two porcelain mugs. Steam trickled from the spout of the kettle, but it hadn't begun its whistling yet.

"Care for honey?" Penelope asked.

"Yeah...thanks. So, pretty neat," he said, pointing to the framed letters. "I was right. You're talented. But anyone with ears can hear that."

"We don't get as many ears these nights," Penelope admitted.

Trevor shrugged. "More music for me. Kinda like I'm getting my own private concert from you."

Trevor mentally kicked himself for coming out with a line like that. The last thing he wanted to be was creepy, but he was doing a fine job of it. Still, he had made it through her apartment door, so he supposed he wasn't off to a bad start.

"I keep them there as a reminder," she replied, pointing to the framed letters."I'd be proud too. Congrats," he said.

Her lack of enthusiasm took Trevor off guard. "Mind if I ask...why are you playing downstairs in your father's bar when you've got free rides to places like that?"

Penelope opened her mouth to respond. He had put her on the spot, and now, he felt guilty about it.

"Sometimes talent comes with a price," she said. Suddenly, the kettle began to whistle. "One sec."

She raced back into the kitchen, switching off the stove, picking the kettle up by the handle and pouring both mugs full of hot water. She bobbed the teabags in the steaming liquid for a moment after setting the kettle back on the stove. Taking a bottle of honey down from the cupboard, she squeezed a bit into Trevor's tea and carried the mugs into the living room. Trevor bridged the gap between them, taking the steaming mug she offered him.

"Thank you," he said.

"You're welcome."

The two of them sat down on the floral-patterned couch. Trevor sunk into it. Despite it being out of the Goodwill catalog, the couch was comfortable. Broken in. He took a drink of his tea while he mulled over what to say next.

"So, you were saying...talent comes with a price," Trevor spoke, taking another sip of tea.

"I have responsibilities, Trevor. My father...he needs my help. He's been doing this a while," she said. "Between you and me, he can't really manage Longitude by himself anymore. This place would fold without me."

"Wow...that's really good of you. I had a feeling you were a good person. I think I could hear it in your music...but I could also hear sadness."

Trevor took a large drink of his tea. Penelope sipped hers. A silence pervaded the room. The hush was palpable, like a piano string stretched between them.

"You listen more closely than the others," she finally spoke. "I could see that after the first few nights. You're special. You understand the music."

"You have graduate school to thank for that," Trevor responded. "Music's been my life for the last several years."

He took one more sip of tea, leaned sideways to set the mug down, and felt his equilibrium shift, almost missing the end table with the cup. As he tried to straighten, he felt dizzy, and his eyelids began to feel heavy.

"I'm sorry...I'm, uhhh, kinda sleepy. It's been a long day, and it's...it's getting late," Trevor said.

Penelope set her tea aside. Trevor blinked his eyes rapidly, trying to clear his vision, but Penelope's pretty face grew blurry. He tried to stand up. His feet felt heavy—like they were stuck to the carpet. Barely had he lifted himself from the couch when he collapsed back onto it.

"Don't worry," she cooed. "It's not you. It's the drugs. Just relax. You'll be asleep before you know it."

Penelope stood up as Trevor's body sloughed sideways. He was barely able to keep his eyes open now, and he couldn't move. The last thing his mind registered before unconsciousness took him was the hazy image of the piano girl he so adored opening the door and letting someone with a distinct limp into the apartment.

When Trevor awakened, it felt like he had only been asleep for moments, but he immediately wished he was back in dreamland and where he lay now was, in fact, pure fantasy. Sadly, from the pain racking his body, it was reality. A reality fraught with nightmares.

He tried to move but was halted by the bite of his bonds. Wincing, he finally forced himself to relax his muscles, at least until he knew more about his situation. The first thing he noticed, when he felt a freezing draft of air, was that he had been stripped of his clothes. His teeth chattered. He could barely move his head due to the heavy metalcollar around his neck. It was bolted to the floor, rendering his escape impossible. The smell of mildew and rot bombarded his nose. He could feel the cold crosshatching of a metal grate beneath his body. A draft of air funneled up between his legs, making his muscles clench.

He was lying on the floor of a drafty old cellar. Frost collected on the green limestone walls. Old wooden support beams sprouted from floor to ceiling. The mortar between the stone was crumbling. Stagnant water stood in low-lying areas of the floor. Four large iron-framed lanterns hung on rings at the four corners of the chamber, casting as many shadows as beams.

If the collar was not enough, he was also lashed to the metal grate by long strands of piano wire connected between two iron rails fastened into the stone floor on the left and right of the massive square grate. They stretched across the grate, pinning him down from forehead to ankles, on the verge of lacerating his flesh with any further pressure. Lengths of wire were looped around his wrists and ankles. A web of steel strands.

"Don't struggle," Penelope's voice cautioned him from the darkness. "You'll cut yourself and wake them up before we have a chance to talk."

"What the hell's going on? What are you doing?!" Trevor asked. "Wait...what do you mean *wake them up*?"

Penelope padded over to him, her bare feet slapping the cold, wet limestone. The grate jostled a bit as she stepped onto it, crouching beside Trevor's head. She leaned over him so he could get a good view of her in the eldritch light. She was now wearing a brown butcher's apron over her black dress and stained leather work gloves.

"It's like I told you," Penelope began. "My father...he can't manage this place alone. He doesn't have the stomach for it anymore. The responsibility falls on me to do what has to be done. To make sure they're sated." Penelope paused, her deep brown eyes growing glassy and watery as she stared into the darkness. "For that, I'm sorry, Trevor."

"Sated? What the fuck are you talking about?!" Trevor shouted. "Let me go! Right now!"

Penelope clamped a hand over his mouth in between a wire that had begun to draw blood on the cleft of his chin and one running just beneath his nose.

"Shhhh," she whispered.

A sharp bang on the grate below echoed through the cellar. The impact sent tremors through the metal, radiating across Trevor's body. The rattle of heavy padlocks reverberated as the grate was struck again.

"Well, you've done it now," Penelope said solemnly. "Now they won't shut up until they're fed."

"They?"

"I don't really know what they are," Penelope admitted. "My grandfather was their shepherd for so long. My mother did it with my father until she took ill and passed. It's just him and me now. But always, there was the warning in my great-great-great grandfather's journal: *If they are released, their plague shall end the world.* It's been passed down from family member to family member."

"You're crazy," Trevor hissed. "I thought you liked me."

"I do like you," she responded, her voice getting wishy-washy with the tears that had begun to run down her cheeks. "I don't want to do this, Trevor. I have to do it. It's you or the world."

Penelope knelt and leaned over, planting a kiss on his forehead. Trevor was right. Her lips were soft. For an instant, he couldn't feel the pain. With another loud bang, the grate shook, snapping him back to his fate. Penelope still hovered over him.

"You were wrong. I'm not the white keys. I wish I were. I love that you saw me that way, but I'm not pure and even; I'm sharp and flat... I'm the black keys." Penelope squeezed his bound hand. "I'm sorry."

She stood up. There was urgency in her movements now. She retreated to one of the rails where the wires were connected. On the rail were many tiny, flanged knobs to which the wire ends were fastened. Trevor looked on, helpless and in horror, as she twisted one knob after another, tightening the wires stretched over his naked body. Their tiny razor-like lengths cut into his skin, drawing blood and provoking a scream.

"I'm sorry it can't be quick. I really am. The...creatures below. They must have their fill of suffering before their meal. The spawn of the night...they need blood, yes, but they need entertainment too."

Penelope circled around to the other rail and tightened the knobs, the wires biting further into Trevor's skin. The loops around his wrists and ankles garroted his flesh, opening up circular incisions. He screamed and his involuntary jerks and squirming only made the wires cut deeper. Blood ran from the thin lacerations, dripping down through the openings in the grate.

Trevor's eyes were half blinded with blood leaking down his forehead, but he could see Penelope leave the rails and move to a space behind his head where an old upright piano sat. There, she sat down and pulled up the bench in front of the instrument. She reached up and flipped on a tiny reading lamp sitting atop the piano.

"Try to enjoy the music," she whimpered. "It's all I can offer you."

Penelope began to play. The tones of Camille Saint-Saens's "Dance Macabre" haunted Trevor as he began to get sleepy again despite his paralyzing pain. With tears filling Penelope's eyes, her fingers floated over the keys. She had played Trevor like an instrument, and the audience below stirred with approval.

Morgan Chalfant is a writer, poet, gamer, and an instructor of writing at Fort Hays State University. He is a native of Hill City, Kansas. He is the author of the urban fantasy novel, *Ghosts of Glory*. You can find him on Instagram: @eyesonly34.

THE WAITING COLD

KATHLEEN PALM

The faceless snowman and its two companions stare somehow.

At the yard covered in white. At the trees that exist at its edges. At me.

Winter is quiet. Too quiet.

It infects me.

I pat more snow on a snowman, wincing at the way my wet glove slaps against it.

No. Not snow*men*.

"Snow people." My words become a puff in the air. That's what Poppy called them when she begged me to go outside and play, to build...no, she said *to see* the snow people.

I readjust my coat, unease creeping over my thoughts at how the mounds of snow stand so still, so silent. How I stand just as still, just as silent. With a huff, I beat snow from my gloves and look anywhere but those snow...people. Poppy went to find the snow people clothes. Maybe they won't be so creepy with colorful hats and scarves.

Maybe the world won't be so blank...meaningless.

Like the empty spot in the driveway behind my gray car. Lonely. Waiting.

For her.

I can almost hear the crunch-squeal of tires in the snow. I can almost see Kim's bright green truck sitting in the white, see her smile as she waves some new purchase for the house, see her joy and strength in her eyes. She makes me better. Makes me whole.

If I stare long enough, maybe she will come back.

She can't be gone.

Above me, the bright blue sky promises a release from the cold and snow and nothingness, though it's a promise I don't believe.

The cold will last forever wrapped around this place. Our place.

Our two-story gray house huddles in the snow.

Our dream. We worked so hard to get this house. *This* one.

Ours...

Crunch.

Crunch.

"Poppy?" I expect to see the tiny five-year-old in her bright green snowsuit, grinning her crooked smile and struggling through the snow.

But there's only the house and the bare trees that surround it. "You're hearing things." I tug my scarf from my face.

Crunch.

"Hello?"

I pull my hat from my head, leaning into the breeze where words drift like dreams. Voices. But there are only trees and snow and emptiness. The next house is a mile away. That's why we chose this place. Our house in the woods.

The forest creaks, branches waving. Clumps of snow fall with soft thwumps. The wind fades.

Again, the sound of footsteps, closer.

I squint into the shadows of the trees. There is someone.

I can hear them talking...whispering.

"Momma!"

My body stiffens, my heart thundering. I spin around, pressing my hand to my chest.

Poppy wobbles across the snow in her too-big boots. Her scarf drags behind her. Her brown eyes shine. She stumbles, then falls to the ground, then flops onto her back, and flails her arms and legs. "Snow people."

"You mean you're making a snow angel." I exhale a cloud of fear and turn from the trees and the snow and the emptiness. I return to the little family of snow people.

"Nope. They're people."

"Then they should have eyes." I press my fingers into their heads to make dents, which makes them look creepier. "I thought you were getting them clothes to keep warm."

"The snow people told me that they like the cold." Poppy sits up and stares at the trees. Her head tilts...like she's listening. "They need it." Her eyes lose focus, her hands go limp in her lap.

"Poppy?"

She giggles, then hops up and runs to the trees.

"Poppy!" I told Kim that we'd have to put up a fence. I told her kids like to explore, but Kim, she... I strangle the thoughts and race after her.

Poppy stops well before the trees. I sigh in relief, coming up beside her and reaching for her hand. "Let's go inside, huh?"

She tugs her hand free of mine. "In a minute."

"In a—"

"Hi." Poppy's voice is bright, her smile giant, her eyes glimmering in the light of winter. She tilts her head and sways.

"Who are you talking to?" Though I shouldn't ask.

"The snow people." Poppy faces me, her mouth twisting in disappointment.

"Right," I say.

Since Poppy started speaking, she's talked to empty corners and dark closets and unoccupied seats. She's talked to Billy and Sue and Mark and Vivian.

But never snow people.

Kids and their imaginations.

Though, Kim believed it was something else, because Poppy talks about books she couldn't have read, about events from long in the past, about ideas too big for her tiny mind.

My dear wife who believed in faeries and magic...who made me believe in everything.

She can't be gone.

A giggle sends icy shivers up my spine.

I stiffen, wrapping my arms around my shoulders and gazing at our daughter, who is staring into space. "What's funny, Poppy?"

"The snow people walk funny, Momma." She giggles again, shuffling forward until her toes are inches from...footprints.

A line of them, one set like someone walked out of the trees and, unless they took the time to walk back in the same prints, they're still there.

"Thank you," Poppy says with a sniff as she wipes her hand across her nose.

I will myself to see the person that must be standing there.

"Yeah. I live here now. Me and Momma and..." She lets her words fade, as she pulls at her mittens.

And my mind fills in what she was going to say: Mommy. Kim.

She should be here. The thought cuts across my heart like sharp blades. I squeeze my hands into fists. She would have built an army of snow people for Poppy.

"Yeah. I know." Poppy gazes up at her invisible friend and frowns.

My hands shake as I reach for her.

"For what?" Poppy scrunches her face in what could be worry. She continues to stare at nothing, shifting from one foot to the other. "I...don't know."

The words. The way she speaks. The way she chews on her lip. It makes me squirm, makes my heart beat in worry.

I place my hand on Poppy's shoulder. "Let's go inside."

She nods slowly, then turns to me and blinks. "Okay." With a hop, she heads to the house.

I turn back to the footprints. Weird. And weird is not something I want to deal with. I have to deal with dinner later and the laundry...

And tomorrow.

And the next day.

Meals and playtime and work.

Again, and again.

The same thing over and over, like a recording stuck in a loop.

Pressure on my arm. Cold. Icy touch on my neck, like fingers.

And a breeze, a whisper, a word.

Wait.

I slap at the air around me, then spin to see that nothing is behind me. Only the footprints. Ones that shouldn't be there.

If only it was Kim...coming home.

I bound through the snow to catch up to Poppy, who's singing a song about snow and cold and waiting.

That word sits in my mind like a knife. Wait.

She stomps up the steps to the back deck and slides open the back door with a grunt of effort. "They know about the accident."

She leaps inside and takes a seat on the floor, wrestling her hands free from her mittens.

I stand in the doorway, stunned. Accident. "What?" The memory of the phone call creeps out from the dark of my mind.

She drops her scarf and mittens on the gray tile kitchen floor, then reaches for her boots. "They know Mommy died." Her little voice is solid and matter-of-fact.

"She's not..." The final word freezes like ice in my throat. Dead. She's not...

There's only blurry memories...a disconnected part of me, floating around in my brain...of a dim room, of flowers, of people crying.

I didn't cry.

They're wrong. They made a mistake.

She can't be gone. I lean against the door frame. Inexplicable fear cascades over my thoughts, holding me in place.

Poppy is a flurry of clothes and messy brown curls. "Come on, Momma. You can't stay out in the cold forever!"

Crunch.

The sound echoes in my head, adding to the uneasiness that still sits in my thoughts. I turn around. Because what if it's...

There's the snow-covered deck, the yard, the trees shivering in the distance, the blue of the sky. The quiet.

Because she might be gone.

I enter the kitchen and shut the door on the emptiness, then lean against the dark wood cabinets. Running my hands over my face, I try to erase a harsh voice that I think has been with me for days, one I won't listen to.

I push myself away from the cabinets and kick off my boots. Poppy will want a snack. I have laundry to do.

Poppy stands and slithers her way out of her snowsuit. "The snow people asked me to tell you that they're waiting." She tosses her wet clothes in a corner and blinks at me. Her gaze holds innocence...and something else. Worry. Or maybe just interest.

"For what?" I don't want to ask, not really. The last thing I want to know is why the snow people are waiting.

"Forever." Her voice is soft, a whisper.

The word fills my head, then drifts through my core. Forever feels...cold and empty.

Uncertain.

I hang coats on hooks, set boots on the rug.

I glance at the unpacked boxes on the table. Kim's coffee maker and mugs. I'm saving them...for her.

Because she can't be gone.

Only...

Poppy stands and shoves her hands in her pockets. "They want you to stay with them."

I drop the mittens before I can hang them to dry. "What does that mean?" I don't know why I ask. I don't want to know. I want this whole conversation to end. I want the footprints in the snow to disappear.

Her chin trembles. She rocks onto her toes, then her heels. "I don't know."

"Silly snow people don't know anything." My voice quivers with fear and doubt. I brush my palms over my thighs and clap my hands. "Why don't you go play, and I'll go do laundry."

Because this is what we do.

With arms flailing, Poppy runs into the living room and falls into a pile of toys.

I step carefully over the doll clothes and accessories that cover the flowered living room rug. Poppy chatters as she brushes plastic hair and picks out a new dress for her friend.

I climb the creaky stairs, stairs we were going to refinish. I run my finger over a few cracks in the walls, walls we were going to paint wonderful colors.

But now, I'll live with stained white walls. I'll live with the cracks.

I still expect to see her. To hear her voice.

But I won't.

I think I know that.

The hall blurs as I shuffle down it, tripping over my own feet.

I head to our room, to the overfull laundry basket. The bookshelf remains an empty shell. That purple sheet set we loved so much never made it onto the bed. A pile of boxes huddles in the corner. Kim's stuff. Cold light trickles in from the window, touching the dusty cardboard, holding them in its frozen touch.

I can't move. I can't do anything. Can't unpack them. Can't get rid of them.

I pull my gaze from the remnants of Kim to the window and the blanket of white outside, to the cold and frozen world that echoes my thoughts.

I blink, squinting at what looks like footprints. Prints that come out of the woods at the front of the house.

Just like in the backyard, like someone is standing there.

Snow people.

I shake my head, wiping my palms over my eyes. Poppy and her imaginary friends. I'm tired. I'm overwhelmed.

I back away from the window and set my hand on the bedpost, solid, real. Out the other window, trees sit in a dark line.

And more tracks.

Some kind of joke. I kick the laundry as I rush out of the room. The window at the end of the hall gets closer and closer. I can see them, the prints. I stop, slamming my hands on the glass. Not just one set, but three.

Surrounded. Trapped.

I rub at the spot on my arm where I felt the cold, at the back of my neck where something touched me.

Maybe we should run. Kim would know what to do.

"Hey, Poppy..." I head down the stairs and stop at the bottom.

Her toys remain scattered around the floor, abandoned, but Poppy's not there.

"Poppy?"

Silence.

The woods. I told Kim that those trees would be trouble. Except I'm not worried about the trees, but what's in them, what's coming out of them. I leap over the toys and rush into the kitchen.

Poppy stands at the backdoor, her face squashed against the glass.

I run my hands over my face in relief. "Poppy?"

She doesn't move.

"Poppy!"

"There are so many." Her voice is low and full of intrigue.

"So many?"

"Snow people. They keep coming."

"Why? What do they want?"

"I told you, Momma." She drags her fingers down the glass with a squeak. She turns with a sigh. "You."

"Me?"

"They say you're like them."

"Well, I..." I try to laugh, though it comes out as a nervous squawk. "I'm not."

Poppy frowns, her face covered in questions.

I look out the door at the snow that glitters in the sun. There are more footprints. They're getting closer.

"That's enough of that game, okay? Let's...let's..." Kim would know what to do, what to say. She would be brilliant. She was always brilliant, coming up with games and crafts, telling magical stories, and making us all feel safe.

And loved.

All I can do is stand here and stammer.

Poppy taps her fingers on the glass. "Can I watch cartoons?"

"Sure." I approach the back door, placing my hands on the glass just as Poppy did.

Her footsteps pound on the floor, then stop. Bright, happy sounds come from the living room. Poppy chatters to the TV, which chatters back.

I scan the backyard. They can't be footprints. The snow is melting and that's causing these...indentations.

That's all. Not snow people.

But what if they are footprints? What if there are snow people? Just standing. Waiting.

Because Kim always said that Poppy knew things.

I reach for the door handle. I can go see. Go prove that there's nothing there.

But the sound of the snow crunching echoes in my head. The memory of the cold touch lingers. I back away, hitting the kitchen table, which shudders and creaks. The boxes shiver, the top of one popping open.

I skirt the table. Kim's things. All waiting.

For her.

Because she can't be gone.

Only...

"The laundry. I was doing the laundry." I wander out of the kitchen, through the living room, then up the stairs. I stop at the top, trapped by the view.

So many tracks. Evenly spaced. They're closer now. I go from room to room, from window to window. The house is surrounded.

I end up in our bedroom, kneeling by the window next to the pile of boxes.

Kim's clothes. Her books. Her collection of animal-shaped candles.

Waiting for her.

The glass is cold against my forehead.

And when I blink, more footprints appear.

So close now.

But patches of grass peek through the blanket of white, erasing the prints. The faint glow of sunset tints what's left of the snow orange.

"Momma! I'm hungry!" The voice crawls into my brain.

"Dinner. Right." I stand, pushing myself away from the window and wandering downstairs.

Trapped. An endless loop of cooking and playing and work.

Poppy's splayed on the floor, kicking her feet. Happy tunes come from the TV. She pushes herself to her knees. "Momma?" Her voice drips with worry, with a trembling tone of what could be fear.

I step over her toys, rub my hand over my face, and cross from the wood floor to the tile. "How about a sandwich?" Though Kim would make something wonderful, something better.

The light fades as I stand at the counter, spreading peanut butter over bread. I drop the knife. I can't see where they are...the footprints.

I hand Poppy her sandwich and go to the back door.

The yard becomes a gray blur. My reflection stares blankly as I stare into the nothing. The flicker of light from the TV creeps through the room. A faraway voice tugs at my brain.

"Momma?"

I don't move. I can't move.

"I'm tired," Poppy's voice is soft.

Kim would have taken care of her. She would have read the right stories and sung the right songs.

"Okay." I lean against the door. I'm tired, too.

Tired of waiting to figure out what's next, to become...someone else. Someone who isn't so unsure.

But I don't know how. And maybe I don't want to.

So I lurk at the door, afraid that I will see something out in the dark and afraid I won't. I can't see the tracks. But they're there. Getting closer.

Night settles in, and I slide down until I'm sitting on the floor. My shoulder presses against the glass. The low murmur of the TV drifts in the background.

I have to watch for the snow people. I think they're there.

Something is there.

And it isn't Kim, is it?

My mind falls in and out of sleep. Images of Kim haunt me in that space. Her bright smile. Her spiky red hair. Her beautiful green eyes. She's coming home. It's her making tracks in the yard.

It wasn't her we buried. There was a mistake. She's coming home.

I blink my eyes open. My cheek is smashed against the door, my breath fogging the glass.

My hands sit limp in my lap. And I sit. Because I don't know what else to do.

The sun creeps up over the world.

With a gasp, I crawl to my feet. The snow is gone. I can't see where they are, the snow people.

A little cloud appears on the other side of the door. A puff of breath.

"Hello?" My voice is a whisper, as insubstantial as that puff.

Spots of fog dot the glass. Marks cut through it, like fingers being dragged down the glass.

Waiting.

I hear it. A tiny frozen word.

Waiting. But not for me. *With* me.

I reach for the handle. To go out. I can't be alone. Can't face a life of uncertainty. Can't be trapped here.

"Momma?"

Poppy.

My shaking hand hovers near the door.

Poppy sits up on the couch and rubs her eyes. Her hair sticks to her face in a tangled mess.

I'm not alone.

"She isn't coming back," I say. The words become heavy. Solid. Real.

I collapse to the floor. All the tears I never shed rush forward. All the sadness consumes my mind. It's just me.

Me and Poppy.

"The snow people are leaving," Poppy says, stepping to the door and waving.

I reach for her, placing my hand in hers.

She turns, squeezes my hand, and smiles. "They still walk funny."

Through my tears, I laugh.

Kathleen Palm is a little light, a little dark and a lot weird. She lives in an old (sadly not haunted) house in Indiana, where she watches horror movies, reads spooky books, drinks chocolate milk, and plots how to spread light through the darkness. Her short stories have appeared in Blackberry Blood, A Quaint and Curious Volume of Gothic Tales, Dark Dead Things: Issue 2, and Shortwave Magazine. Her upper middle grade horror trilogy, The Nowhere Series, will be published in 2025-2026 from Undertaker Books. Her middle grade book Nightmare Garden is coming from Watertower Hill Publishing in 2026.

THE COMPANION

THERESA JACOBS

P arker hated the thought of his great-grandmother's last days being wheelchair bound in the musty retirement home, with its frail elderly, and the underlying scent of urine and death. She could no longer see or hear, so he slipped his fingers between her palm and the wheelchair's arm rest. His hand felt like an inferno compared to her cool, satiny skin.

"Are you warm enough?" he yelled.

She gave no indication of his presence as her clouded eyes stayed fixed on the window. He could only assume she knew where the window was by the brighter light from the blinding blanket of falling snow outside.

"Violet's much happier when you're here."

He swiveled, startled by the unexpected voice from behind, and raised a brow at the nurse who'd snuck up on him carrying a tray of food. "How can you tell? She always looks the same when I come."

"Because she doesn't open her eyes for us," she replied, setting the tray onto a small wheeled table, rolling it closer to where Parker sat. "Have you fed her before?"

He noted the nurse's nametag pinned high up near her shoulder. "Thanks, Jane, and no, no one has told me she won't open her eyes. Does she do that for others in the family? I'm usually only able to be here on the weekends." He shrugged, feeling guilty, pulled the table closer and said, "I can feed her."

Jane pursed her lips, unfolded a crisp cotton napkin, and tucked it around Violet's neck. "Oh, yes, of course she does. I didn't mean to imply she only does that with you. I simply meant she looks happiest with visitors."

Parker scooped what he assumed was pureed peas onto the spoon and pressed it against his great-grandmother's lips. Her gaze never strayed from the window, but her lips parted and she gummed the mush without a sound. "Well, I bet she misses her pets, too. Has anyone ever told you she had cats her entire life?"

Jane shook her head, giving him a polite smile.

"Sorry, I'm sure you have other food to deliver."

"Thanks, it was nice to meet you."

Parker smiled back at the nurse. "You too. Say, uh, can I bring in a cat...like a therapy one, I mean. I know they do with dogs."

"No, there are too many people here with cat allergies. Plus, all the loose fur, you know?"

He nodded. "Right, okay thanks, I'll think of something."

After two hours of one-sided conversation, Parker returned home and sprawled across the couch, pulling out his phone. He always honored his great-grandma's time by giving her his full attention when he visited. He saw too many other visitors staring at their phone instead of being present with the people they'd gone to see, and he found it disgusting.

Opening Facebook, he wasn't surprised that the first ad on his page was of a white-haired woman with a cat on her lap.

"They're always listening," he muttered, clicking the ad for *The Purr-fect Companion.* It showed an elderly person holding a stuffed toy cat in their lap, petting it as though it were a real animal. He clicked the attached video. A jaunty tune played as a rotation of happy families awed over *The Purr-fect Companion,* a trainable animatronic cat that could purr, roll over for belly rubs, lift a paw for attention, walk, and meow. He scrolled past the video to read more about the toy and check out the reviews.

"Made in Bangladesh. That's different," he said, impressed with the number of five-star ratings. *It's not the real thing, but will she know that?*

Less than a week later, a large box appeared on his doorstep. Thrilled, Parker opened it and lifted the packing to find a curled ball of orange and white fur. He'd chosen the color of his great-grandmother's all-time favorite cat, Marmalade. Even though she was now blind, it made him feel as if he was honoring her most beloved memories.

The weight and stiffness of the thing surprised him as he removed it from the box. Rubbing his fingers along the belly, back, and legs, he was unable to find any switch and laid it down to read the instructions.

The Purr-fect Companion is a one-of-a-kind voice-activated anima-tronic toy.

COMMANDS:

Wake—activates movement.

Sleep—activates curl up and rest.

Here—activates movement toward voice, with tail motions.

Paw—activates sit with air-pawing motion.

Soft—activates kneading.

Love—activates purring.

Play—activates bowing, tail motions and pawing at ground. Movements may vary.

Petting for 40 seconds will also activate curl up rest and purring before going into full rest mode.

Good thing all she has to do is pet the thing, he thought, setting the cat on the floor and saying, "Wake!"

Gears whirred to life. The cat's head lifted, eyes opening to reveal bright emerald irises. Its legs unfurled with the clicks and pops of mechanical parts realigning themselves. It stood staring at Parker.

"Here," he called, placing his hand down as if it were a real animal. The tail swished across the floor, clicking with each pass as it walked toward him. The stare remained focused on him, and he wondered if there was a camera inside. How creepy would it be if this was like a nanny spy cam? Although what could the elderly possibly reveal? He pushed away the conspiracy rhetoric as the fuzzy pink nose touched his finger and the cat stopped moving.

"Paw," he commanded and couldn't help but laugh when the orange paw lifted directly into his open palm. "Cute. I'm sure Granny will love this," he said, picking it up.

The inside casing was hard plastic and not at all comfortable to the touch, plus it was heavier than he'd anticipated, but he figured if it were lying in her lap, it would be more balanced. Setting it down on his lap, he looked at the instructions again and said, "Soft."

The cat began lifting and pressing its clawless feet against his thighs in the act of kneading. The unyielding plastic jabbed into his thigh muscles. "OW! Stop. Alright we won't tell the staff that function. Sleep."

He watched the unnatural movements as the cat's joints clicked and whirred as it curled up, tucking its head into its chest. He ran his hands over the soft fur, thinking. A gentle vibration tingled through his thighs as the thing began to purr.

"Yeah, this will lift her spirits." Parker set the cat aside until his next visit.

His thoughts swirled from the depth of sleep to consciousness, curious about what time it was in the still-dark room. Pushing his feet over to the cooler, empty side of the bed, Parker didn't feel the urge to urinate and wondered what woke him. From elsewhere in the small apartment, a *thunk* sound drew his attention.

He lifted his head off the pillow, tempted to say "Hello," which would be silly considering that if a thief *had* broken in, they weren't likely to engage in conversation. He listened with intent and every other common noise sounded louder than usual. The fridge started up with a clank, the hum an annoyance at the moment. Next, the heat vent emitted its whoosh of warm air. Outside, a lone car crunched over the hard-packed road, obscuring all other sounds until an unusual noise caught his ear.

He cocked his head, rolled his legs slowly off the bed, and leaned forward to discern what it could be.

A low, consistent *ERR-ERR-ERR* pattern prattled on.

Parker reached between his bed and nightstand, wrapping his hand around the handle of a baseball bat he kept there. He took two swift steps to the doorway and out into the hall.

His heart jolted into arrhythmia as two glowing green eyes appeared between the hall entranceway and the living room. They disappeared briefly before reappearing. The creature remained stock still.

He paused too, bat held high, and wracked his brain trying to understand what this thing was. A racoon? In the apartment, in winter, how? The thing blinked again. Another car came along his street. Its lights gave some additional illumination through the long patio doors, allowing him to see the outline of a furry body with a long tail held straight up.

"Cat?" he whispered.

The eyes vanished and reappeared.

"Sleep," Parker commanded and sure enough, the things joints produced the *ERR* sound as the cat first sat, then curled its head down into its belly.

"Christ, you almost gave me a heart attack," he said, walking toward it before reaching under its belly to lift it. Without any command, the toy came alive in his hand. The cat's front end twisted, catching the flesh of his palm where it connected the back end. He cried out, opening his fingers in surprise and pain.

The cat flew from his hand, hit the floor with a loud thud, and lay still.

"What the fuck is wrong with this thing?" he said, nudging it with his toe. The cat lay still and for some reason Parker remembered the line from the movie *Cool Runnings* and whispered, "Sanka, you dead?"

He chuckled. "Man, you're losing it."

He decided to leave it where it was for the moment and, since he was now wide awake, take the opportunity to go online and check if there were others who'd experienced issues with the animatronics before.

As a bachelor in a small one-bedroom apartment, Parker never bothered with a dining table; instead, he'd set up his forty-two-inch-long desk in the space where most families would gather to eat, along with his two monitors and laptop. He enjoyed gaming in his free time, though his mother constantly pushed for him to settle down with someone. But he loved the freedom to do what he wanted, when he wanted.

Such as now, he thought. If I had a partner, they'd probably be annoyed at my choice to stay up. He smirked at all his friends in relationships and sat, turning on the laptop. He didn't hear the sound of motors whirring from down the hall as he typed in the Google search bar: *Purrfect Companion issues.*

The page was loaded with results from the official sponsored site, to Reddit commentary, to YouTube videos and more. As he scanned the page, trying to decide where to look first, a light *thud-thud-thud* sound came fast from behind. Parker spun in time to see the cat leap into the air from four feet away, aiming directly for him.

Startled, he pushed himself back, arms raised. The wheeled chair whipped across the hard floor, slamming him into the blinds against the patio doors, clanging against the window and entangling him in their folds. The cat, having lost its target, smashed into the laptop, pushing them both with another deafening crash into the wall.

"What the!" Parker screeched as the cat righted itself, scrambling back toward him. Still fighting to escape the blinds, he didn't get his bearings in time as the heavy toy landed with its back paws on his groin, front paws on his chest. His legs came up as the air expelled from his belly. He didn't have a moment to think before the cat's blunt plastic teeth bit into his soft breast tissue.

Parker screamed as flesh was torn from his body and he flung away the cat with all his might. Blood arched a Pollock painting over the room, and himself, as the thing flew through the air and hit the opposite wall, where it dented the plaster before falling to the floor. Its motors whirred and clicked while the legs flayed, trying to find footing.

He slid from the chair onto his knees in order to get away from the suffocating blinds, keeping an eye on the erratic toy where it flopped about, still trying to get itself upright. If not for the blood running down his belly and the throbbing pain he felt, the sight would be extremely funny and gain viral status on TikTok. At this moment, however, he needed to find a suitable object to bust the hardshell open and put an end to the monster. After that, he could contemplate why this happened and how hard he'd go after the company. He couldn't bear the thought of what would have happened had he brought it to his great-grandmother right away.

"Sleep!" he yelled, eyeing the bat he'd set down against the wall. The command had no effect, however, as the thing figured out how to stand again and now crouched in attack mode. Parker stood with knees bent, hoping he was faster, or smarter, than a simple animatronic as he tried to decide between grabbing the bat to the right of the cat, or fake it out and make a run to the left. If he went left, he'd hit the hall and could get back around into the galley kitchen and grab—What, a knife? His mind raced.

The cat leapt.

His choice of actions was taken away.

Parker dove right.

They collided halfway into their motions.

The toy hit Parker on the left side below his ribcage. Its weight and hardshell knocked the air from his lungs and his feet out from under him. The solid laminate floor gave no cushion to his head or bones. He registered a snap that came with blinding pain as something in his shoulder gave and he slid into the chair space under the desk. Without time to process how hurt he was, his left leg suddenly shot forward as the cat wrapped itself around his shin. It felt as though a cement boot had been placed over his lower leg and Parker grunted, trying to roll off the injured shoulder in the tight space.

Time moved both in fast-forward and slow-motion through the unfathomable ordeal. He reached up for the desk surface, needing its support to get free when the cat's teeth sunk deep into his muscle. He shrieked, kicking his leg up, trying to shake the damn thing off. Unable to get out of his position and fight the creature, Parker flipped onto his back. His vision faded to black from the searing pain in his shoulder as it jammed against the side of the desk. He knew if he passed out it'd be game over.

"Fuck!" he hollered, bringing himself back into the moment to discover the thing on his leg was shaking its head back and forth, trying to tear more flesh from his body.

He flung his leg up onto the edge of the desk. There came a satisfying crunch of plastic hitting wood. Shockwaves added to the fire of pain, but he knew he couldn't stop now and bashed it again. Mixed with the noise, the sound of a tiny motor revved and the scent of burning plastic began to fill the room. A loud hammering added to the melee and vaguely

Parker heard the next-door neighbor yelling that they were calling the cops.

Do it! His mind screamed as exhaustion overpowered his adrenaline and he let his leg fall to the floor.

The cat released its grip as flames burst from within, adding a chemical reek to the space.

Coughing, which rattled the bones in his busted shoulder, Parker wriggled out from under the desk. The smoke alarm started its shrill beeping and sirens—presumably from the neighbor's complaint, resounded in the background. He eyed the now-hairless lump of melting plastic as he gave it a wide berth, limping in his boxers out of the apartment and into the fresher air of the main hallway.

Other tenants were either already dressed in haphazard outfits of tossed-on clothes, or simply poking their heads out of their apartments to discern if they actually needed to flee into the cold winter air. One spotted Parker, covered in blood, limping and cradling his bad arm, and closed their door.

"Yeah, thanks," he murmured, hobbling toward the lobby, praying an ambulance was on its way as well.

Three hours later, Parker half dozed under the wonderful influence of pain medications, his arm across his chest in a sling, listening to the ceaseless noise of the hospital's emergency ward. A nearby conversation about an animatronics factory brought him fully awake.

He called out, "Hey?"

A male nurse in purple scrubs and the person in blue ones stopped talking.

"Can I help you?" Purple asked.

"Yeah, what happened in Bangladesh?"

"Oh honey, you have enough happening here." Purple waved his hand in a circular motion. "You can catch the news later."

Shaking his head, Parker said, "No, this may be from that! Did the news have anything to do with toy cats?" He caught a surprised look between the nurses and pressed, "Tell me, please?"

Blue nurse nodded as if resigned and said, "All the machines, including toys went berserk, killing or injuring thousands of people."

Parker tried to sit up and winced at the jolt of pain the medication wasn't strong enough to smother. "How, though? How?"

The nurse in blue rushed forward, pressing their hand on Parker's good shoulder. "Relax sir. They said the factory machinery was contaminated by a virus. It's early, they're still searching for who uploaded it and why. You know how it is these days, probably a disgruntled employee wanting retribution." They shrugged as if the issue was no big deal.

"It's always evil humans," Parker uttered, closing his eyes and barking a laugh. "And here I was worried about A.I."

Exhausted from the medicine and adrenaline crash, he could no longer keep his eyes open. He heard the nurses move on to the next patient and behind their voices a distant television spoke warnings for any *Purr-fect Companion* purchased in 2024 to be destroyed immediately.

Theresa Jacobs entertains readers with her versatile style, from kids' books, to horror, to crime. She'll never let her creativity be stifled. She still works full time in the real world and spends every free moment either writing new stories or binge-watching popular shows. She lives in Canada with her handy husband and goofy dog, both of whom vie for the rest of her time.

SPIRITUAL AWAKENING

RAINIE ZENITH

It was meant to be a place of peace and serenity, but the deeper they drove into the shadowy remoteness of the woods, the more Alyssa Nielsen's sense of disquietude intensified.

She shuddered and pulled out a pocket mirror, absentmindedly checking her reflection, anything to take her mind off an irrational but increasing sense of foreboding.

Zeke plucked the mirror from her hands.

"No you don't," he said, grinning, day-old stubble accentuating the squareness of his jaw. "There are no mirrors at the retreat, and I'd like to keep it that way. We go there to focus on the internal, not the external."

"But how am I supposed to do my makeup?"

"You won't need any makeup. This retreat is about letting go of the body and awakening the spirit."

Alyssa didn't tell him she had at least two more mirrors tucked away in her extensive cosmetics kit buried in her luggage. It was more habit than anything, dragging all that stuff along with her; when you were a top social media influencer, you had to be prepared to touch up for a photo wherever you went.

She sneaked a glance at Zeke's bare arms, toned and tanned, biceps flexing as he gripped the wheel of the van. He had the looks and physique to succeed as an influencer, too, but was far too spiritual to get involved in something so skin deep. Yoga was not just his workout; it was his way of life.

"Yoga's just as much about the meditation as it is about the postures," he said, glancing between Alyssa's face and the dirt road. "The spirit is even more vital than the body."

Until she met Zeke, Alyssa had considered herself a devoted yoga enthusiast. She practiced every day, and her social media presence revolved around images of her lithe body contorted into impossible poses. She enjoyed the influencer lifestyle—all that free sportswear, all those adoring followers, a life of chasing the sun and looking glamorous. But sometimes, certain aspects of it left her feeling a bit hollow—like skipping meals to attain the illusion of a flat belly or taking the same damn shot hundreds of times and still not being satisfied with the result.

She'd been in one of those disheartened moods when she encountered Zeke espousing the benefits of his meditative woodland retreat.

It had seemed like such a good idea at the time, but it probably would have been a better idea to come in summer, Alyssa reflected. Perhaps then the woods might have been a pleasant respite from the sun, with daylight trickling through the leaves like it did in the brochures. Now, at the peak of winter, the woodland was cold and oppressively dark, the thick canopy blocking out what little daylight persisted in the overcast sky.

Alyssa inhaled deeply and exhaled with impatient force. Zeke had warned her the retreat was isolated, but they had been driving through woodland for almost an hour now. How much farther could it be?

With that thought, they passed through a makeshift wooden gate and pulled to a stop beside a single row of unassuming log cabins.

"Here we are—Spiritual Awakening Woodland Retreat. Ninety miles from the nearest civilization. You have to lose yourself before you can truly find yourself."

Zeke winked, climbed from the van, and unloaded Alyssa's flamingo pink suitcase from the back.

"You're staying in Cabin Two," he said, pointing. "Get yourself settled in and be at the Main Cabin in time for the welcome address."

He handed her the case. Its cheery exterior seemed out of place among the rustic cabins and the gloom of the woods.

Alyssa shivered, took her suitcase, and a moment later, tentatively pushed open the door to Cabin Two. It was pitch dark in there and smelled faintly of chai. She fumbled around at the wall for a light switch, finally finding one and igniting a dim glow in the center of the wooden ceiling.

The room was austere, containing only four single beds pushed against the raw timber walls. Alyssa squinted in the half-light and did a double take.

A body lay on one of the beds.

Alyssa's heart leapt into her throat, and she shrieked.

The body jerked upright.

"Hello there."

"Hello," Alyssa stammered above her racing heart. "I'm sorry, I didn't know anyone was in here. You gave me quite a fright."

The other woman was much older than Alyssa, with long silver hair and skin pale as moonlight.

"My apologies. I didn't mean to spook you," she said. "I'm Anahata. The bed by the door is free."

Alyssa tossed her belongings on the sparse mattress, then accompanied Anahata through the biting cold to the Main Cabin, the sixth and final cabin on the row. The older woman's thin white kaftan blew mercilessly in the icy breeze. Alyssa wrapped her thick woolen scarf tighter around her throat, feeling the chill even beneath her blue puffer jacket.

Anahata lifted her skirts to enter the cabin, and Alyssa noticed she was barefoot. *Was she completely impervious to the cold?* Alyssa wondered.

The Main Cabin was several times larger than the other cabins and was filled with conversation. Roughly ten people milled about, all of them dressed in white robes like Anahata's. A woman with white-blonde hair, who Alyssa guessed to be in her thirties, split off from the group and came to greet them.

"This is Alyssa," Anahata said, "and this is Shakti."

"Welcome, Alyssa!" Shakti gushed, shaking the her hand with fingers like slivers of ice. "Are you here just for the weekend?"

"Yes. Was there the option to stay longer?"

She was sure Zeke had only mentioned the weekend retreat.

"Yes, there's a permanent residency option," Shakti smiled.

Alyssa giggled. "That's not quite where I'm at right now. How many of you live here?"

Shakti glanced around the room, and Alyssa followed her gaze around the small crowd, noticing it was made up entirely of women. "All of us except you, actually! But we love having weekenders. Fresh blood is very exciting."

"How long have you lived here?"

"Oh, forever and a day!" Shakti laughed. "Feels like it, anyway."

Silence descended as Zeke swept into the room like a god, confident and reassuring, all masculine energy and black clothing. He launched immediately into an explanation of how the weekend would run, and Alyssa felt embarrassed as she realized this was really only for her sake.

"The weekend retreat is a *spirit-focused* retreat. The use of electronic devices is not permitted, and any items such as phones are to be handed to me now. You can collect them at the retreat's conclusion."

Alyssa reluctantly dug her mobile out of her jeans pocket and passed it to Zeke.

"It is also a silent retreat. From this point on, no one is to speak, save for myself, of course, as I instruct you in our yoga and meditation classes."

Alyssa closed her eyes and sighed. She'd heard about retreats where you weren't allowed to speak before but hadn't realized this was what she'd signed up for. It was going to be a long weekend.

Despite the friendly welcome she'd received, Alyssa's initial feelings of unease continued to grow as the weekend progressed. There was something very odd about the other women. They were so homogenized—all dressed in white, all pale as death, all with strange Sanskrit names, and all lacking in appetite. Saturday's dinner was a thin vegetable soup, and while Alyssa couldn't seem to fill up on it no matter how much she ate, the other women all seemed to barely touch theirs.

Then again, it was probably expected that they would develop similar quirks, living together as they did in isolation from the rest of society. Zeke spent only his weekends there; he was city based during the week. Alyssa wondered if any of the women ever went into town, but of course, she couldn't ask them. The silence rule was strictly in force, with no one but Zeke uttering so much as a grunt.

This was another factor contributing to her distress. She was surrounded by people but unable to communicate with them, and she had no phone to contact her friends in the outside world. She felt lonely, and the hours of still mind meditation were not helping to keep her mental health in check. She was sure the long periods of silence were causing her to hear things that weren't there: muffled whispers, distant shrieks.

Plus, the showers were cold. She had been so looking forward to a nice warm shower before bed but instead had to shiver her way through a trickle of ice water. If she was going to take one thing away from this retreat, it would be a renewed appreciation for the small things in life.

Sunday morning, she woke early and sneaked a mirror out of her case, facing the wall to check her reflection so that her body obscured the contraband item. It was a good thing she did because she heard Anahata wake and leave her bed. Alyssa angled the mirror to see if the older woman was looking her way but couldn't find her in the mirror's reflection. She heard the door handle turn and angled the mirror accordingly. She watched the door open, heard the exiting footsteps, and watched the door close.

Anahata was not visible in the mirror at all.

Alyssa stuffed the mirror back in her case with a shaking hand. All this meditation was sending her bonkers. First, hearing things that weren't there, then, not seeing things that *should* be there. She decided to skip the morning meditation and go for a walk in the woods instead.

She dressed in her warmest thermals and beanie, but the freezing morning air still crept through and chilled her to the bone as she took a step into the thick woodland shadows. Mist hung in the air like a cobweb, like a warning sign. It was too dark; she might get lost. She contented herself with doing laps of the cabins.

On her third circuit, she noticed a strange collection of objects shining out of the darkness behind the Main Cabin. She stepped closer and tried to discern what they were.

Little crosses, maybe a dozen of them; little painted white crosses impaling the earth like daggers in a dartboard.

A pet cemetery, perhaps?

Alyssa bent to her knees and saw words on the crosses, names handwritten in black text.

Wendy Sachs.

That didn't sound like a pet name.

Helen Chinnery.

What was this? Crude memorials?

Alyssa Nielsen.

Alyssa recoiled, saucer eyed, covering her mouth and nose with her hands.

Her name. On a cross. Why?

Why?

Screw the silence rule. She had to know the meaning of this.

She ran from the hair-raising little crosses, rounded the corner of the Main Cabin, and saw Zeke striding down the steps.

"Zeke!"

He frowned and shot a finger to his lips.

"No, I need to talk to you! Now."

He registered the wild panic in her eyes.

"Alyssa, what's wrong?"

She took him by the hand, dragged him behind the cabin to the collection of crosses, and pointed at the one with her name on it.

"What is this? What does it mean?"

Zeke smiled at her as though humoring a five-year-old.

"Dear Alyssa, please calm yourself," he said. "Everyone who completes the weekend retreat is gifted with a spiritual name at the closing ceremony. Their former name is placed on a cross here as a kind of memorial, if you will, to the person they were prior. It's symbolic, you see."

Alyssa felt her heartbeat reduce speed by a fraction. That would explain why the women all had names like Anahata and Shakti. They weren't their real names. They were spiritual names. Their real names were written on the crosses out here.

"You'll receive your spiritual name at the closing ceremony this afternoon," he said. "Now come on, Alyssa. It's time for the mid-morning yoga class. And I expect complete silence from you until the closing ceremony."

#

Alyssa was beginning to doubt her own sanity. Zeke's explanation of spiritual names had made perfect sense, and she'd enjoyed the relaxing yoga class, a nourishing Buddha bowl, and a surprisingly interesting lecture on ethics. Why, then, did she still feel such bloodcurdling dread? After all, there was only the closing ceremony to go before Zeke would hand back her much-missed phone and drive her out of this cursed woodland, back to her city apartment.

The ever-present knowledge that she was ninety miles deep in the dark woods played at the edges of her thoughts. So did the unexplained incident of Anahata failing to appear in the mirror. And even though she now understood the reasoning behind the crosses in the ground, there was still something creepy about the whole idea. Maybe it was meant to be symbolic of the name change, but in Alyssa's mind, it was what you did when the person died.

She entered the Main Cabin and sighed with relief that the silence rule was finally at an end. The women were all chatting excitedly, and Alyssa stood awkwardly at the perimeter, trying to find her place in the conversation.

"It's been so long," Shakti was saying. "I can't wait!"

"I know," Anahata said. "Zeke's chosen well."

Before Alyssa could figure out what they were talking about, Zeke swept in with the authority of a ship's captain, a white robe draped over one arm, a golden chalice in his hand.

The crowd fell silent as he addressed them.

"Here we are already, time for our closing ceremony," he said. "And I would like to reinforce what I hope you have learned from this weekend: the spirit is more important than the body. I call on Alyssa Nielsen to come and receive her new spiritual name."

The eyes of the pale women glittered with excitement as they turned expectantly to Alyssa. She stepped forward, swallowing the lump in her throat. Something was tugging at the corner of her brain, trying to tell her something. Something was wrong. But what was it?

He handed her the white robe and gestured for her to put it on. She pulled it over her jacket and jeans. He passed her the chalice, which was filled with a liquid the color of blood and the odor of bitter almond.

"With the drinking of this celebratory wine, we shall lay the name Alyssa Nielsen to rest and bestow upon you your spiritual name."

Zeke gestured for Alyssa to drink. She sniffed the bitter potion and balked. Its acerbic scent screamed of danger.

She took a mouthful.

"And so, we lay your body to rest, thus awakening your spirit. Release the body, Alyssa, and move into the spirit realm."

Alyssa spat the liquid back into the chalice, spit again, wiped her mouth.

"Lay my body to rest? It's poison, isn't it?"

"Alyssa, you're being irrational," Zeke said. "This is a yoga retreat, and that is a glass of non-alcoholic wine."

Alyssa wasn't listening. She glanced wildly at the women in white, those pale women, each of whom had a little memorial cross in the ground. Those pale women who didn't seem to eat or feel the cold. Those pale women who had no reflections. Alyssa realized with a horrified jolt that those women were ghosts.

Spirits.

Zeke wanted to turn her into a spirit, too.

"Come on, Alyssa, you're not getting into the *spirit* of things," Anahata jeered.

The crowd of women moved closer.

Alyssa felt her breathing stop.

"Drink the wine," Zeke said quietly, chillingly.

Alyssa hurled the goblet into the crowd of women and fled through the confusion, out of the cabin, into the woods. Branches snapped at her wrists and ankles, but she didn't dare stop—not until she had run so hard, and so far, she simply had to.

She slumped down against a cold, damp tree trunk and listened for signs she'd been followed, but the only sound that rang in the still dark night was her labored breath.

As her breathing quieted and her body returned to resting temperature, the chill of the night set about trying to pierce her protective layers with its prongs of ice air. She started walking; in what direction, she didn't know. Ninety miles from civilization, deathly cold, with no food or water.

She stopped and held her head in her hands, then snapped to attention at a faint sound on the horizon.

"Alyssa? Alyssa?"

It was Zeke's voice carrying on the chill breeze.

"Alyssa, come back before you die of exposure."

To die of exposure and pass to the beyond, or to die of poison and be one of Zeke's spirit women?

That was the only question.

Writing pieces that often fall within the gothic fantasy realm, Rainie Zenith's work has been published in numerous literary journals and short story anthologies. She was the winner of the 2020 Monash Short Story Competition and the Fountain 2020-2021 Essay Contest. She enjoys blurring the boundaries between reality and perception, and her current project is a gothic psychedelic novel.

GARBAGE DAY

L.S. KUNZ

G loria liked garbage day. She had worried moving to a retirement community would be a mistake. But her new trash bin had wheels. Wheels! And there was always the possibility of running into a neighbor at the end of the driveway. A chance to say hi. Maybe even chat.

Slipping into the down parka Michael had given her last month for Christmas, Gloria wedged the door to the attached garage open with her heel and dumped the trash into the bin. Used tissues and yogurt cups tumbled out in a tiny blizzard and settled on the bottom of the bin like a dusting of snow. An old lady living alone didn't generate much waste.

After depositing the empty trash can in the mudroom and checking that the doorknob was unlocked, she pulled the door closed behind her and pushed the garage door button. With a snap and a whir, the single-car garage door retracted. She'd been in her new house two weeks already, but the attached garage still gave her a thrill. Her whole life she'd had to scrape her windshield on cold winter mornings. Now, her sedan had its own room. Like a housemate.

Michael had convinced her to move to the retirement community. She had fretted that it would be too expensive, but he had offered to pay what she couldn't. Said he wanted her to have the best of everything. Of course he had. Such a good son.

As the garage door clicked into place, a cold wind kissed Gloria's cheeks. Made her eyes water. She blinked the tears away and noticed how dark it was. Oh dear. Time must have gotten away from her while she had been watching Jessica Fletcher catch another murderer. What time was it? Not even eight, surely. But with Daylight Savings Time, it might as well have been midnight. Black as an abandoned *Murder, She Wrote* set out there.

Gloria massaged her knuckles. They hated the cold now. Maybe she should wait till morning. No. It would be as dark then as now. That was winter for you. Best to be done with it.

Tugging the bin away from the wall, Gloria tipped it onto its wheels and maneuvered it around her sedan and out onto the shoveled and salted driveway. The garage lights cast double shadows on the cement, gifting her two companions for her chilly walk—the first, her own shadow, a squat version of herself that matched her stride for stride; the second, her shadow's shadow, a hazy outline that always seemed to be a step ahead. Like a premonition.

When Gloria rounded the bend, the garage lights disappeared behind the side of the bungalow and the snow-capped branches of a Bosnian pine.

Gloria stopped. Let the trash bin tip back to its resting position. Her shadow friends were gone. She was alone in the dark. Haloed in a cloud of her own breath. Without the rumble of the wheels, a winter hush enveloped her. Silence so complete it threatened to conjure up the joy of Christmases past.

Should she turn back? Jessica Fletcher was waiting inside. Paused mid-sentence. A knowing look on her guileless face. Missing garbage day wouldn't be the end of the world. The bin wasn't even half full.

No, Jessica Fletcher wouldn't quit, and neither would she. Her eyes were adjusting to the dark. The streetlamps along the sidewalk provided ambient light. And a crescent moon was just smiling out from behind the distant mountain peaks like a bashful new friend. In its silvery glow, the patches of ice on the driveway glistened like ornaments fallen from a Christmas tree.

Gloria tipped the trash bin back onto its wheels. By the light of the moon, she trundled between shiny sheets of ice and parked the bin at the curb. Done.

Before heading back, she paused. Maybe she wasn't the only resident who had lost track of time while streaming a show on the new flatscreen TV their son had bought for them.

Rubbing warmth back into her hands, Gloria looked left and right. Not a soul. Every fifty feet or so, lonely streetlamps punched holes in the dark. In their hazy glow, she glimpsed a shoveled sidewalk. A mailbox. A bare tree. No neighbors smiled her way. No one waved hello.

Gloria sighed. It wasn't like she was alone. Michael had promised to stop by soon. And Jessica Fletcher was waiting back at the house. But it would have been nice to say hello to someone tonight. Someone who would say hello back.

Tucking her hands into her parka pockets, she turned back toward the bungalow. As she did, from the corner of her eye, she caught a flash of white.

She stopped. Was someone there after all? Her heart skipped. Maybe a neighbor was walking over to say hello?

She blinked at the darkness. Waited.

There it was again. Nearer this time.

A flash of white two streetlamps away.

Gloria raised her hand to wave.

But her hand stopped mid-greeting.

Something wasn't right.

It was a person. She could tell by the stride. But the person wasn't on the sidewalk. Wasn't strolling in and out of the streetlamp lights.

The person was... No. Couldn't be. It must have been a trick of the light.

Gloria blinked again. But the sight didn't shift.

The person was walking down the center of the street. Barely a shadow in the outer reach of the streetlamp's glow.

Gloria stepped back. She didn't know why.

Why was someone walking down the middle of the road? Didn't they know how dangerous that was?

In the fuzzy lamplight, the figure came briefly into focus. Shoulder-length hair. A woman? No. The hair was stringy and flat. The gait cocky. A young man. Walking fast. Long strides in the dark. The kind of strides that come with fisted hands.

Gloria couldn't tell if his hands were fisted, but she could tell something was off.

He wore all white. White t-shirt tucked into pleated white shorts. White tube socks in white sneakers. No coat. No hat. Nothing protecting his bony white knees from the bitter cold. White t-shirt. White shorts. The only contrasting color in his outfit were the two dark stripes running the length of his t-shirt. Suspenders.

He was wearing suspenders. Like a clown.

Gloria took another step back.

The young man wasn't slowing down. If anything, he was speeding up. Walking with purpose. Toward her house. Toward her.

Gloria wanted to shrug it off.

This was a safe neighborhood. Gated. That's why Michael had picked it. She had a panic button hanging around her neck. But when she reached for it, it wasn't there. She had taken it off to do the dishes.

She was alone.

Alone. And a stranger was striding toward her.

A stranger in white. In the middle of winter. In the middle of the street. In a hurry.

Gloria didn't want to say hello anymore. Turning, she scuttled up the driveway. She didn't run. What would the neighbors think? But she didn't walk either. What if the stranger was following her? Gaining on her?

She glanced back. Didn't see anyone.

Somehow, that made it worse.

At the Bosnian pine, she rounded the bend and rushed headlong into the mixed blessing of the garage lights. She could see. But she could be seen. A bullseye on her back.

Crouching like an escaped convict caught in a searchlight, she sprinted into the garage. She felt like a lumbering ox. What would the neighbors think?

She skirted her sedan, ignoring the lightning strikes of pain firing from her knees, and slammed the garage door button.

The garage door rumbled to life. Started its descent. Before, she had found the door's speed a marvel. Now, it was maddeningly slow. Too slow. If the stranger wanted to get in before the door closed, it would be all too easy.

Eyes glued on the shrinking gap between the descending door and the ground, Gloria felt for the doorknob and turned it, ready to dive inside if she saw so much as a shadow.

The garage door clicked closed. Gloria gasped. Safe at last.

Only when she'd gotten inside and turned the deadbolt did she realize she was shaking like a broken massage chair. Resting her forehead on the doorframe, she breathed in and out.

In and out.

She was safe. Everything was okay.

Wait. Was the front door locked? The back?

She was moving again. Running on wobbly knees.

In her mind, she could see it. The front door standing ajar. A gaping black hole. But when she turned the corner, the door was shut tight. She checked the lock. Bolted. Thank goodness. Without pausing, she ran for the back door. Locked tight as well. For good measure, she double-checked the front door. Still locked. Everything was secure.

Leaning on the front door, she caught her breath. Waited for her hands to stop shaking.

She was being silly. This was a safe neighborhood. Whoever the kid in the street was, he was no threat to her. Just a visiting grandson out for an evening stroll.

In suspenders.

Did young folks wear suspenders nowadays? Should she buy a pair for Michael?

What a spectacle she had made of herself. Fleeing from nothing. She'd be the talk of the neighborhood in the morning. Old Gloria Campbell, scared of her own shadow.

No matter. A laugh at her expense would liven up the place.

In the meantime, Jessica Fletcher beckoned. She'd just close the blinds first. Ward off any peeping Toms. Secure the house for the night.

Against the darkness, the windows were mirrors. In each pane, her own withered face confronted her. Shrunken like in a funhouse mirror. Or maybe she really did look that small. Was this how other people saw her? She averted her eyes and twisted the blinds shut.

When she got to the front room, the glow of the porch light through the front window was a relief. She didn't have to look at her own shrunken image. And she could see that her front porch was empty. No one there.

With a spin of the wand, she shut the last blind.

There. Safe and secure. Now, back to Jessica Fletcher.

Gloria hesitated. Turned back.

She had closed the blinds so the slats tilted down. Maybe they should tilt up. That way, if anyone peeked in, the most they could see was the ceiling.

Good idea.

She twirled the wand.

The blinds opened onto the front porch.

But it wasn't empty anymore.

Outside the window was a face staring in.

For a second, Gloria's brain told her it was nothing to worry about. Her own reflection looking back at her.

But the front porch was lit. And this was not her face.

Unlike her face, it was smiling.

The energy drained from Gloria's body like a ghost departing. Her brain couldn't process the whole image. Just parts.

Forest green suspenders.

Wide, lipless grin.

Hard, blue eyes. White teeth.

Tilted head.

Gloria's hand was still on the wand. It kept twisting.

The blinds closed. The image disappeared.

A whimper escaped her lips.

She reached for her panic button. It still wasn't there.

She took a breath. No one was outside. It was just her imagination. No more watching *Murder, She Wrote* reruns after dark.

With one trembling finger, she lifted a slat. Peeked outside.

The face was still there.

Grinning.

And now there was a noise. A high-pitched whine. Scraping.

Gloria stooped and peeked out a slat near the bottom of the window.

Just beyond the glass, she saw the young man's hand. As she had suspected, it was fisted.

Fisted around something long and sharp and shiny.

A carving knife.

He was scraping the tip of the blade on the window pane.

Two dots and a crescent moon grin.

A smiley face.

Gloria dropped the slat. Stumbled back as if the stranger might leap through the glass. Fled into the kitchen, arms flailing for her panic button. Her phone. Anything to summon help.

She called Michael first. He told her to call 911.

The police and Michael arrived at the same time.

Together, they broke the silence. Filled it with motion. Action. Purpose.

Every light in the house was on. Gloria's bungalow glowed like a beacon. Michael sat on the couch beside her and held her hand. His hand was strong. Competent. Tan from the Hawaiian vacation he had taken his wife and kids on. It had been Gloria's lifelong dream to go to Hawaii. She was so glad her son had finally been able to go.

Around her, authoritative voices filled the silence. Inside the bungalow, badges checked every nook and cranny where a stranger might hide. Outside, red and blue lights pulsed in the darkness, and flashlights probed the bushes. The young man in suspenders was nowhere to be found. Chased off into the night, no doubt.

Finally, when the bungalow was cleared and the yard secured, Officer Tibbits sat in the floral chair across from Gloria and asked her questions. What did he look like? How old? How tall? What did he weigh? Did he have tattoos? Other markings? What was he wearing?

Gloria answered Officer Tibbits's questions as well as she could. Even the one about the clothing. Even though it made her hands shake all over again.

When she told about the knife scraping the window, Officer Tibbits nodded at another uniform, who dusted the window for fingerprints. Didn't find any. Didn't even find a scratch from the blade. It was like the stranger had never been there at all.

But he had. Gloria had seen him. Could see him still.

His cold, smiling eyes. His suspenders stark as two prison bars against his white shirt.

She would never forget him.

When the police started packing up, Gloria's panic returned. She pressed her hands together, but it didn't help.

Her arms shook so violently she couldn't steady the herbal tea Michael had steeped for her. When she lifted it to her lips, she sloshed steaming liquid over the rim, and Michael took it back again. Grabbed a paper towel to wipe up the floor.

"Mom," he said. "Do you need me to stay here tonight?"

The words were like magic. As soon as Michael spoke them, the trembling faded into memory as fast as a herd of wild horses.

Gloria grasped her son's hand. Her Michael. Such a good boy.

But when Michael lifted her hand and saw it was steady, he smiled. "That's better. You don't need me here at all, do you."

It wasn't a question. The tremor crept back into Gloria's hand, but she pulled it away so Michael wouldn't notice.

Michael gathered his things. Coat. Cellphone. Car keys. "I have a deposition starting at eight in the morning. Best be off."

A flurry of barked orders and shuffled papers and the bungalow was empty. Gloria was alone. Again. And it wasn't even nine p.m.

Michael didn't call the next day. Or the day after. On the third day, the phone rang, but it was the police, wanting to know if there had been any additional unwanted visitors.

No, no unwanted visitors. No visitors at all.

Gloria watched Jessica Fletcher and went for walks around the neighborhood. Neighbors waved hello, but none had time to chat. They were visiting with family or listening to headphones or cleaning up doggie doo-doo.

She walked to the swimming pool and found it locked up tight for winter. At the playground, she found grandparents gushing about grandchildren on the swings and slide.

She walked home, opened a can of soup, and turned on *Murder, She Wrote*.

The HOA fees came due, and Michael paid them electronically. Such a good son.

By the time garbage day rolled around again, the stranger in suspenders had nearly disappeared into distant memory. Nearly. Gloria still had a tinge of fear, so she made sure to take the trash down before dinner.

The sun was a cold orb hanging in the sky like one of those new-fangled LED bulbs. Bright enough to blind, but no warmth at all. The grass was brown and frozen. The trees bare. But it was light outside, and that was what mattered.

Gloria parked the trash bin at the end of the drive and scanned the street for a neighbor to say hello to. It had been a week, and no one had so much as mentioned the police cars at her house. The flashing red and blues. The searching flashlights. It was like the stranger had never been there at all.

Wandering back up the drive and back inside, Gloria watched the garage door close till it clicked shut and then she checked that all the doors were locked. She was safe for the night.

Another serving of soup—the can labeled it minestrone, but it tasted like the others—but no *Murder, She Wrote*. Nothing scary after dark.

At dusk, Gloria closed the blinds. Ever since the stranger, she closed the blinds before it got dark. She didn't want to see her own shriveled reflection in the window and wonder if it was her or someone else.

Starting in the kitchen, she circled the house, leaving the front room for last. She didn't like to go in the front room anymore. She would have left those blinds closed forever, but they were the only windows facing the street. What would people say?

When she reached the front room, the porch lights were on, and the porch was empty. Only then—when she saw the unoccupied front porch—did she realize her heart was racing. Quick as a lizard, she darted across the room, grabbed up the wand, and spun the blinds closed.

There.

Safe as a child hiding under the covers.

If the young man was there, she'd never know it.

To prove it to herself, she peeked.

Lifting one slat, she peered out with one eye and saw two eyes peering back. Blue eyes. Crinkled in the corners from grinning.

Gloria dropped the slat.

How could a smile be so malevolent?

Like a kid picking at a scab, she couldn't leave it alone. With one finger, she lifted the slat, and there he was again. The stranger. This time, holding the shiny blade straight up, so it split his sinister smile in two.

Gloria dropped the slat and reached for the panic button. It was there this time. She would never take it off again.

One click and fifteen minutes of pacing summoned the police. Michael was thirty seconds behind. As before, Michael held her hand as the officers spread out. They walked the block. Scanned every yard and searched every hiding place. They found nothing.

Gloria gripped Michael's hand. It was dry, rigid.

"How did the deposition go?"

"What?"

Michael looked distracted.

"The deposition. How did it go?"

"Fine. We're working out a settlement. I had to leave the negotiations to be here."

Gloria's throat constricted. She had promised herself she would never be a burden.

Letting go of Michael's hand, she patted her hair.

"I didn't mean to interrupt. The police are here. You can head back if you need to."

Michael mostly suppressed an eye roll. Took her hand back. Pulled her toward the couch.

"Sit down. Tell me what's going on."

Gloria sat, confused.

"What's going on?"

Michael nodded. "Is there really a stranger?"

Gloria swallowed. Her mouth felt as dry as Michael's hand.

"What?"

Michael didn't manage to suppress the eye roll this time.

"Are you making him up?"

Gloria sat up. Tried to muster some dignity. But no matter how straight she sat, Michael's tailored suit still made her robe and slippers feel old and shabby.

"Of course he's real. Why would I make him up?"

Michael stretched his neck one way and then the other. Under his Hawaiian tan, he looked as worn out as her robe.

"I don't know. Are you lonely? Is that what's going on? You want me to visit more?"

Gloria snatched her hand away. Rested it in her own lap.

"What are you saying?"

Michael sighed. Rubbed his eyes.

"I don't know, Mom. A stranger who shows up on garbage day in shorts and suspenders threatens you with a knife, but doesn't try to come in. Doesn't bust down a door or break a window. Doesn't even knock. It all sounds pretty preposterous."

Not sure what else to do, Gloria averted her eyes. Perched on the couch cushion like a chastised child. She felt ridiculous, and that was worse than feeling afraid.

Then the police were there. Officer Tibbits again.

"There's no one out there. No signs that anyone was ever there. Is it possible you imagined him? After a scare like you had last week, the mind can play tricks on you."

Officer Tibbits and Michael exchanged a look that told Gloria all she needed to know.

Sitting up so straight her back ached, she looked at the floor and spoke the words everyone expected of her.

"I really believed he was there."

That was the ticket. The invitation for everyone to pack up and get back to their lives. That was what they had wanted all along, and they were at it almost before she had finished her sentence.

When Gloria was alone again, she turned on *Murder, She Wrote*. It didn't matter if she scared herself before bed tonight. She wasn't going to sleep anyway, and she needed to see a friendly face.

When garbage day rolled around again, Gloria collected the trash and rolled it down to the curb. She went down while it was still light out, and she didn't look right or left. She scuttled back up the drive and watched the garage door all the way down till it clicked closed.

Back in the house, she closed all the blinds and checked all the doors. No sunset for her. She was shut up tight and would stay that way till morning. It didn't matter if she looked unfriendly. No one would notice anyway.

She opened a can of vegetable soup for dinner and ate it in front of the television.

After a couple episodes of *Murder, She Wrote*, it was eight o'clock. Showtime.

Gloria turned down the volume on the television. What if the stranger decided to break in this week? What if she pressed the panic button and no one came? The old lady who cried wolf?

When eight-thirty came and went without so much as a squeak, Gloria got restless. What if she missed him? What if he decided not to come back?

Gloria jumped to her feet and rushed to the front window.

Grabbing the wand, Gloria spun the blinds open, and there he was. Head tilted. Grin wide and sinister. Green suspenders stark as two knife slashes down the front of white fabric.

Relief boiled up Gloria's torso. Her lips curved into a smile.

She lifted her hand and waved.

The stranger didn't blink. Didn't acknowledge her presence at all except to lift one hand, the one with the knife, unfurl three fingers, and wave back.

Gloria closed the blinds again and returned to *Murder, She Wrote*.

She liked garbage day. It was nice having a visitor to look forward to.

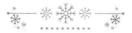

L.S. Kunz lives in northern Utah with her husband. She is a member of the League of Utah Writers and has received local awards for her short stories and middle grade fiction. Her work has appeared in *Ellery Queen Mystery Magazine*, *Baubles From Bones*, and *Utah's Best Poetry & Prose 2023*.

WINTER'S LULLABY

DITA DOW

The wind howled through the pine branches, carrying a flurry of snow that bit at Evelyn's exposed cheeks. She pulled her scarf tighter, squinting against the whiteout conditions as she trudged up the winding path to the cabin. Behind her, Thomas struggled with their luggage, his breaths coming out in ragged puffs.

"Are you sure this is the right place?" he called out, his voice nearly lost in the gale.

Evelyn paused, fishing out her phone. The screen was dark—dead battery. She cursed under her breath. "It has to be," she shouted back. "The rental company said it was the only cabin for miles."

As if on cue, a structure materialized out of the swirling snow. It was larger than Evelyn had expected—a two-story log cabin with a wide, sloped roof. Icicles hung from the overhangs like jagged teeth. The logs were weathered and dark, as though the place had been standing against the elements for centuries.

"Oh, thank God," Thomas muttered as they approached the porch. He dropped the bags and fumbled in his pocket for the key while Evelyn stamped her feet, trying to regain some feeling in her toes. The lock clicked, and the door swung open with a harsh scrape that echoed in the stillness of the cabin.

The interior was dark and cold, smelling faintly of pine and something else—something musty and unpleasant. Evelyn wrinkled her nose. Thomas dropped their bags and felt around for a light switch. A single bulb flickered to life, casting long shadows across the living room.

"Cozy," he said with forced cheerfulness. "I still can't believe you found this place."

"It was a great deal. The rental agent said it's been vacant for years, but they assured me it's in perfect condition."

Thomas raised an eyebrow, "And you didn't think that was...odd? A place like this, empty for so long?"

"People can be superstitious about remote cabins, Thomas. Besides, it's quiet, secluded. We needed that."

"I know. I just hope there's no catch."

Evelyn moved farther into the living room, her boots leaving wet prints on the hardwood floor. A massive stone fireplace dominated one wall. Above the fireplace hung an enormous set of antlers, and she shuddered, wondering what gigantic beast could have sported such a rack.

"I'll get a fire going," Thomas said, moving to the hearth and kneeling to light the prepared kindling. "Why don't you check out the rest of the place?"

Evelyn nodded absently, her gaze still fixed on the antlers. As she turned away, a strange thought crept in—had they just moved? She glanced back, heart skipping for a moment, but there they were, lifeless as ever.

Must've been her imagination.

The kitchen was small but well equipped, with modern appliances that seemed at odds with the rustic decor. Evelyn opened the refrigerator, finding it stocked with the groceries they had requested.

She was about to head upstairs when a sound stopped her in her tracks. It was faint, barely audible over the crackling of the fire, but unmistakable: a child's laughter.

"Thomas?" she called out, her voice tight. "Did you hear that?"

"Hear what?" he replied from the living room.

Evelyn shook her head. "Nothing. Never mind."

She climbed the stairs slowly, each step creaking beneath her weight. The upper floor was cloaked in shadows, the air colder and stagnant, as if time had stalled. Three closed doors lined the narrow hallway. Evelyn hesitated, the silence pressing in, before reaching for the nearest knob, her hand trembling.

The bedroom beyond was spacious, dominated by a king-size bed draped in a quilt that looked undisturbed for years. Dim light filtered through the window, casting strange patterns on the floor. Frost crept over the glass, swirling like ghostly fingers. For a moment, her breath caught—a face seemed to form in the frost, pale and hollow eyed. She blinked, and it was gone, leaving only the frost behind.

Evelyn backed out, moving to the next door. This room was smaller, cramped with a twin bed and a worn wooden dresser.

Finally, she turned to the last door, the coldest one of all. It creaked as she nudged it open to reveal a tiny bathroom.

"Everything okay up there?" Thomas called from downstairs.

Evelyn took a deep breath, steadying herself. "Yeah," she replied, hating how shaky her voice sounded. "Everything's fine."

But as she turned to leave the room, the nagging sense that everything was far from fine refused to leave her.

Evelyn descended the stairs. She found Thomas still in the living room, stoking the fire. The flames cast a warm glow across his face but did little to dispel the chill that had settled in her bones.

"Hey," he said, looking up at her with a forced smile. "How's it look up there?"

Evelyn hesitated, unsure of how much to share. "It's... fine. Spacious. But Thomas, don't you think it's a bit odd? This place, I mean."

Thomas straightened, his brow furrowing. "Odd how?"

"I don't know. It just feels...off. And I could have sworn I heard—" She broke off, shaking her head. "Never mind. It's probably just my imagination running wild."

Thomas crossed the room and placed his hands on her shoulders. "Eve, look at me. We needed this getaway, remember? After everything that happened with—"

"Don't," Evelyn cut him off. "Please, let's not talk about that."

A flicker of hurt crossed Thomas's face, but he nodded. "Okay. I'm sorry. Why don't we unpack, and then I'll make us some hot cocoa? We can curl up by the fire, just like we used to."

Evelyn managed a small smile. "That sounds nice."

As they unpacked, Evelyn tried to shake off her unease. She told herself it was just the stress of the past few months, just the grief that still clung to her like a second skin. But every creak of the floorboards, every whistle of wind through the eaves, set her nerves on edge.

Night fell quickly, the darkness outside absolute. Evelyn found herself avoiding the windows, unable to shake the feeling that something was out there, watching.

They sat on the couch, mugs of cocoa warming their hands. Thomas had found an old radio and tuned it to a station playing soft jazz, the music tinny but comforting in its familiarity.

"So," Thomas said, breaking the silence that had stretched between them. "Do you want to talk about it?"

Evelyn stiffened. "Talk about what?"

"You know what, Eve. The real reason we're here. Dr. Rosenberg thought it would be good for us to—"

"To what?" Evelyn snapped, setting her mug down with more force than necessary. "To 'get away from it all?' To 'reconnect?' As if a weekend in the woods could fix everything?"

Thomas sighed, running a hand through his hair. "That's not fair, Eve. I'm trying here. We both are. But you have to meet me halfway."

Evelyn stood abruptly, pacing the room. "I can't do this right now, Thomas. I'm tired. I think I'm going to turn in."

As she headed for the stairs, the radio suddenly emitted a burst of static, making them both jump. Through the white noise, Evelyn could have sworn she heard a child's voice, sing-songing: *"Come play with me."*

"Did you hear that?" she gasped, whirling to face Thomas.

He was frowning at the radio, fiddling with the dial. "Hear what? It's just interference. Probably the storm."

Evelyn opened her mouth to argue, then thought better of it. She persuaded herself she was just tired, her mind was playing tricks on her, that's all it was.

"Right," she said quietly. "The storm. Goodnight, Thomas."

She climbed the stairs slowly, feeling the weight of Thomas's gaze on her back. In the bedroom, Evelyn changed quickly, shivering in the cold air. As she slipped under the heavy quilt, her eyes were drawn to the window.

The frost patterns seemed to have grown more intricate, forming what looked like reaching hands. And there, in the center of the glass, was a perfect handprint, small like a child's.

Evelyn squeezed her eyes shut, her heart pounding. When she opened them again, the handprint was gone.

Sleep was a long time coming, and when it did, Evelyn's dreams were plagued by the sound of childish laughter and the sensation of icy fingers brushing against her skin.

* * *

She awoke with a start, the room pitch black around her. For a moment, she was disoriented, unsure of where she was. Then it all came rushing back—the cabin, the storm, the strange noises.

Beside her, Thomas slept soundly, his breathing deep and even. Evelyn envied him his peace. She was about to go back to sleep when she heard it: a soft thump from downstairs, followed by the unmistakable sound of footsteps.

Evelyn's breath caught in her throat. She reached out and shook Thomas's shoulder.

"Thomas," she whispered urgently. "Thomas, wake up. There's someone in the house."

Thomas stirred, mumbling incoherently. The footsteps grew louder, now accompanied by a soft, rhythmic squeaking, like someone climbing the stairs.

"Thomas!" Evelyn hissed, louder this time.

He bolted upright, instantly alert. "What? What is it?"

"Listen," Evelyn breathed.

They sat in tense silence, straining their ears. The footsteps had stopped, but the squeaking continued, punctuated by what sounded like quiet giggling.

Thomas reached for the bedside lamp, but when he flicked the switch, nothing happened.

"Power's out," he muttered.

He fumbled for his phone, using its dim light to illuminate the room. "Stay here," he told Evelyn, his voice low. "I'll go check it out."

"No!" Evelyn grabbed his arm. "We should call for help."

Thomas shook his head. "No signal, remember? We're on our own out here."

The wind outside howled, rattling the windows. Evelyn shuddered, pulling the quilt tighter around herself. Thomas slid out of bed, moving cautiously toward the door. Evelyn watched, her heart in her throat, as he eased it open and peered out into the hallway.

For a long moment, there was nothing but silence. Then, suddenly, a high-pitched laugh echoed through the house, followed by the slamming of a door.

Thomas jumped back, nearly dropping his phone. "What the hell was that?"

Evelyn was already out of bed, grabbing for her clothes. "We need to get out of here. Now."

They dressed hurriedly, neither daring to speak. As they crept down the stairs, Evelyn's mind raced. This couldn't be happening. It had to be a dream, a hallucination, anything but real.

The living room was eerily still, the fire nothing but glowing embers. In the faint light, Evelyn could make out something on the floor: a trail of wet footprints, too small to be either of theirs, leading from the front door to the base of the stairs.

Thomas saw them, too. He opened his mouth to speak but gasped when a child's voice sang out from somewhere in the darkness: *"Ring around the rosie, pocket full of posies..."*

Evelyn clapped a hand over her mouth to stifle a scream. Thomas grabbed her arm, pulling her toward the front door.

"Ashes, ashes..."

They fumbled with the lock, hands shaking. Outside, the storm raged, snow and wind lashing at their faces as they stumbled onto the porch.

"We all fall down!"

The voice, filled with malevolent glee, came from right behind them. Evelyn turned, catching a glimpse of a small, pale figure with hollow eyes before Thomas yanked her forward.

They plunged into the snow, struggling against the wind. Evelyn's lungs burned with each icy breath, her legs already growing numb.

"The car," Thomas shouted over the howling gale. "We need to get to the car!"

But as they reached the end of the path, Evelyn's heart sank. Where their car should have been was nothing but an empty expanse of snow.

"No," she moaned. "No, no, no..."

Thomas spun in a circle, desperately searching for any sign of the vehicle. "This is impossible," he muttered. "It was right here. It has to be here!"

A giggle floated on the wind, and Evelyn turned to see a childlike figure standing in the cabin doorway, backlit by a pulsing blue glow.

"Come back inside," it called, its voice simultaneously sweet and terrifying. *"Don't you want to play?"*

Evelyn clutched Thomas's arm. "Run," she whispered. "Just run."

They plunged into the dark forest, the child's laughter echoing behind them as their cabin disappeared into the storm.

The forest was a maze of shadows and swirling snow. Evelyn and Thomas stumbled blindly through the darkness, branches whipping at their faces, roots threatening to trip them with every step. The wind howled through the trees, carrying with it the faint, haunting echo of childish giggles.

"We can't keep going like this," Thomas gasped, his words barely audible over the wind. "We'll freeze to death out here."

Evelyn knew he was right, but the thought of going back to that cabin filled her with a primal terror. "We can't go back," she panted. "You saw...you heard..."

Thomas grabbed her arm, pulling her to a stop. In the dim moonlight filtering through the clouds, Evelyn could see the fear in his eyes, but also a determination that had been missing for months. "Eve, listen to me. Whatever's happening, we're in this together. Okay? Just like always."

For a moment, Evelyn felt a flicker of the old connection between them, a warmth that had nothing to do with exertion. She nodded, squeezing his hand.

A twig snapped nearby, and they both whirled toward the sound. Through the falling snow, Evelyn caught a glimpse of a small, darting figure.

"There!" Thomas shouted, pointing in the opposite direction. Another childlike shape flitted between the trees, giggling. How many of them were there?

They were surrounded.

"This way!" Evelyn tugged Thomas's hand, pulling him toward a gap in the encircling figures. They ran, snow crunching under their feet, branches scraping their skin.

Suddenly, the ground dropped away beneath them. Evelyn felt a moment of weightlessness before they were tumbling down a steep slope, snow and rocks and branches all blurring together in a painful jumble.

They came to a stop at the bottom, bruised and disoriented. Evelyn lay still for a moment, the world spinning around her. She tasted blood in her mouth.

"Thomas?" she croaked, struggling to sit up. "Thomas, are you okay?"

A groan answered her from a few feet away. "I'm alive," Thomas muttered. "Though I'm not sure that's a good thing right now."

As Evelyn's eyes adjusted to the gloom, she realized they had fallen into some sort of ravine. Steep walls rose on either side, the tops lost in the swirling snow. Ahead, the ravine curved out of sight.

"We have to keep moving," Evelyn said, forcing herself to her feet. Every part of her body ached, and she was pretty sure she had sprained her wrist in the fall.

Thomas nodded, wincing as he stood. "Any idea where we are?"

Evelyn shook her head. They were hopelessly lost, with no idea which direction would lead them back to civilization.

They made their way along the ravine, the walls providing some shelter from the wind but deepening the shadows around them. Evelyn couldn't shake the feeling they were being herded, driven toward some unknown destination by the unseen presences lurking in the forest above.

After what felt like hours, the ravine widened into a small clearing. Evelyn's heart skipped a beat when she saw what stood in the center: an old, dilapidated church.

Its steeple was crooked, listing dangerously to one side. The windows were dark, empty sockets, and the door hung askew on rusted hinges. Snow had drifted against its walls, softening its edges but unable to mask the aura of abandonment and decay.

"What the hell?" Thomas whispered. "How is this here?"

Evelyn shook her head, unable to tear her eyes away from the building. It felt wrong, like a prop on a movie set, utterly out of place in the middle of this forsaken wilderness.

A gust of wind cut through the clearing, and with it came a sound that made Evelyn's blood run cold: the tinkling notes of a music box, playing a distorted version of "Ring Around the Rosie."

"We should go," Evelyn said, her voice tight with fear. "We need to find another way."

But as she turned, she saw the path they had come from was now blocked. Where the ravine had been was a solid wall of rock and ice. They were trapped.

The music grew louder, seeming to come from inside the church. And then, carried on the wind, came a voice—a woman's voice, filled with a desperate, pleading edge that struck a chord deep within Evelyn's soul.

"Help me," it called. *"Please, help my baby!"*

Thomas grabbed Evelyn's arm. "Eve, no. It's a trick. It has to be."

But Evelyn wasn't listening. That voice... It was impossible, and yet she recognized it instantly—it was her own.

Before Thomas could stop her, Evelyn was running toward the church. She reached the door, its paint peeling and wood rotting, and hesitated for just a moment before pushing it open.

The interior of the church was cloaked in shadow, the pews barely visible in the gloom. At the far end, where an altar should have been, stood an ornate crib. The music box melody grew louder, filling the air with its eerie tune.

Evelyn approached slowly, her heart pounding. As she drew closer, she could make out a small figure lying in the crib, swaddled in blankets.

"Eve, don't!" Thomas called from the doorway, but his voice seemed to come from very far away.

Evelyn reached the crib and peered inside. For a moment, all she saw was a bundle of cloth. Then, slowly, it began to move. A tiny hand emerged, reaching up toward her face.

With trembling fingers, Evelyn pulled back the blanket, revealing the face beneath. Her breath caught in her throat as she stared into a pair of familiar eyes—eyes she had last seen closed forever in a hospital room six months ago.

"Sophie?" Evelyn whispered, tears streaming down her face. "Oh God, Sophie, is it really you?"

The baby gurgled, a sound that was at once heart-achingly familiar and subtly wrong. As Evelyn watched, the child's features began to shift, melting and reforming like wax held too close to a flame.

Evelyn tried to step back, to run, but found herself frozen in place. The baby—the thing that had been a baby—sat up, its body elongating, limbs twisting into impossible angles. Its mouth opened in a wide, toothless grin that split its face nearly in half.

"Mommy," it said in a voice that was decidedly not a child's, "don't you want to play with me?"

Evelyn screamed, the sound tearing from her throat and echoing through the empty church. She felt hands grabbing her shoulders, pulling her back, and then she was falling, falling into darkness...

*   *   *   *

"Evelyn! Eve, wake up!"

Evelyn's eyes snapped open, her heart racing. She was back in the cabin bedroom, tangled in sweat-soaked sheets. Thomas was leaning over her, his face etched with concern.

"It's okay," he soothed, helping her sit up. "It was just a nightmare."

Evelyn looked around wildly, half-expecting to see the grotesque baby-thing lurking in the shadows. But there was nothing—just the unfamiliar bedroom, bathed in the pale light of dawn filtering through the frost-covered windows.

"It felt so real," she whispered, her voice hoarse. "The church, the baby...Sophie."

Thomas's face fell at the mention of their daughter's name. He sat on the edge of the bed, taking Evelyn's hand in his. "I know," he said softly. "I dream about her too sometimes."

For a moment, they sat in silence, the weight of their shared grief hanging between them. Evelyn squeezed Thomas's hand. "I'm sorry," she said. "For pushing you away. For agreeing to come here when I knew I wasn't ready."

Thomas shook his head. "No, I'm the one who should be sorry. I thought...I don't know what I thought. That a change of scenery would magically fix everything?"

A bitter laugh escaped Evelyn's lips. "Some change of scenery. This place is—" She broke off, a chill running down her spine as she remembered the events of the night before. "Thomas, last night...did we..."

"Did we what?" Thomas asked, his brow furrowing in concern.

Evelyn swallowed hard. "Go out...in the storm?"

"No, we went to bed, and as far as I know, we stayed here all night," Thomas replied, his voice tinged with worry. "You probably had a nightmare."

Evelyn frowned. It had felt so real—the fear, the cold, the pain of their fall. She could still hear the music box melody playing in the back of her mind. "I think we should leave," she said abruptly. "I know we're supposed to stay the weekend, but I can't... I don't think I can be here anymore."

To her surprise, Thomas nodded readily. "I think you're right. This place—it's not good for us. Too isolated, too... I don't know. There's something off about it."

They packed quickly, neither of them wanting to spend any more time in the cabin than necessary. As Evelyn zipped up her bag, she glanced at the window. The frost patterns seemed to swirl and dance, and for a moment, she could have sworn she saw a child's face peering in at her. She blinked, and it was gone.

"Thomas, don't you feel it?" she murmured. "This place... it's like it's alive. It's feeding off us."

Thomas froze mid-motion, frowning. "Feeding off us? Eve, listen to yourself. It's just a cabin—a creepy one, sure, but—"

"It's not just a cabin!" Evelyn interrupted, her voice raw. She wrapped her arms tightly around herself as though warding off an unseen force. "It's like it knows us—what we're afraid of. The laughter, the dreams, the way it shifts. It's not random, Thomas. It's—" She hesitated, her throat tight. "It's hunting us."

Thomas's expression wavered, his confidence cracking. "Eve, we're stressed. We're exhausted. This place is weird, sure, but—"

"No, you felt it too," Evelyn said, her voice dropping to a whisper. "I've seen the way you look around, like you're waiting for something to jump out of the shadows. This place wants us afraid, Thomas. The more scared we are, the stronger it gets."

Outside, the world was transformed. The storm had passed, leaving behind a landscape blanketed in pristine white snow. Their car was where they had left it, though it took some effort to brush off the thick layer of snow that had accumulated overnight.

As Thomas loaded their bags into the trunk, Evelyn took one last look at the cabin. In the clear light of day, it looked almost picturesque—a cozy winter retreat straight out of a postcard.

"Ready to go?" Thomas asked, coming up beside her.

Evelyn nodded, turning away from the cabin. As they climbed into the car, a movement in one of the upstairs windows caught her eye. A hollow-eyed face stared through the frost, a pale hand leaving its imprint on the cold glass.

Evelyn's breath caught in her throat and she slammed her car door shut. "Thomas," she began, but he was already starting the engine, the radio coming to life with a burst of static.

Through the white noise, Evelyn heard a child's voice, sing-songing: *"Come back soon. We'll be waiting..."*

"Did you hear that?" she gasped, turning to Thomas.

But he was focused on navigating the snow-covered driveway, the radio now playing an innocuous pop song. "Hear what?" he asked, glancing at her.

Evelyn looked back at the cabin one last time as they pulled away. The window was empty now, no sign of the handprint or the figure.

As they drove down the mountain, the cabin's ghostly whispers fading behind them, Evelyn finally broke free from its suffocating grip. She gasped the crisp air, lungs burning. Though the immediate danger faded, grief and terror clung to her—a grim reminder that the cabin's horrors weren't truly left behind.

Dita Dow is a best-selling, award-winning author who creates gripping mysteries, thrillers, and supernatural stories. With over 30 years in law enforcement and private investigations, she brings real-life insight into her characters and plots. Outside of writing, Dita loves hiking, discovering ancient archeological sites, and ex-

ploring the world.

SILVER SHOT

BRITTNI BRINN

T he plain of snow remains untouched, a gleaming pane of diamond glass under the full moon's spotlight glow.

I take a sip of coffee. Bad batch from the gas station down the highway, tastes like cigarette water. But it's all there is and I choke it down, watching the empty winter field through the windshield of my dodgy second-hand car. I need this job, I remind myself. The late hours, the bad coffee, the shitty car with a broken heater—it's worth it, in the end. And to be fair, I only have to do this part once a month.

Movement on the snow. It's still far off, but I know a werewolf when I see one. Heading this way—drawn to the promise of the city, the smells of cooked food, discarded take-out, human blood. I don't know why they always come through this field. Probably a den of them, far into the interior where the trees crowd like broken teeth.

I fumble with my gloves, unbuttoning the wool covers to leave my fingers bare. The werewolf takes its time, loping over the snow like it's enjoying itself. I load the first silver bullet into the rifle. I slowly roll down the side window and stick my upper body through. My breath goes up in a cloud.

The werewolf slows near the sparse wire fence marking the edge of the field, sniffing the air. Its coat is brilliant white, its eyes black flecks under heavy brows. Teeth as long as butcher knives gleam in the moonlight. Like most werewolves, it travels on all fours—from a distance, some would mistake it for a bear. But I've been doing this a long time.

I take aim just as the werewolf turns my way. It knows. With a roar, it barrels toward my car.

My shoulder takes the kickback. The bullet rips a hole in the werewolf's chest. The delayed retort of the shot echoes across the empty field.

The werewolf stumbles and collapses into the snow.

Dropping down onto the driver's seat, I shoulder the car door open and plough through the crusted snow as fast as I can toward my kill.

The werewolf begins to change.

"Come on, come on," I push myself. Reaching the fence, I lift the top wire and use my boot to press the lower wire into the snow as I duck through.

The beast shrinks. Its teeth recede. Just in time, I pull a tuft of its white fur free.

All that's left is the body of a young woman, her blood leaking red on the snow.

I tuck the fur into my pocket and take a minute to scan the field. Nothing else for miles. Seems like this one was unlucky.

I wrap her in a wool blanket from the trunk of my car. I used tarps early on, 'cause they were easier to get the blood out of, but it didn't feel right. I buy wool blankets in bulk now, so I don't have to reuse them. People deserve a little dignity, when it's all over. I think about that as I drive the deserted highway until I reach the police station.

"Another one?" the inspector asks across the counter.

"Yep."

He motions a couple officers over to collect the body from my car. "You're eleven for eleven this year, Annie."

I hand an officer my keys and slide my hunter's license under the plexiglass barrier. "Do I get a prize if I make it a full twelve?"

"I'll think about it." He stamps my license on the page marked *November*. "Once the medical examiner confirms the body was a werewolf, I'll put your payment through."

He slides my license back and gets to work on a form. I sign at the bottom. The officer returns with my keys.

The cold hits me as I leave the station and digs past my layers into my bones. God, I hate winter. The walkway needs to be salted and I take my time returning to my car, not wanting to add a broken leg to my laundry list of expenses. Could I hunt with a broken leg? I think so. The inspector's teasing about my monthly kill would be in vain if I didn't bag a werewolf to end off the year.

I arrive home in one piece and park in the detached garage. Before going inside, I check the trunk: only a dribble of blood on the rough carpeted interior. I'll clean that up tomorrow. Taking my gun, I cross the narrow yard and unlock the back door of my tiny bungalow.

Not bothering to turn on the kitchen light, I lock the rifle in the gun cabinet and empty my pockets of ammo. I set the tuft of werewolf fur on the table. Then, I head to the bathroom for a shower.

A loud bang wakes me up around six a.m. Rolling over, I lift the curtain from the window next to the bed. The street out front is empty. I wait, but there's no follow up to the noise. Maybe I imagined it.

Exhausted from the long night of staking out the field, it doesn't take me long to fall back asleep.

I get up around ten, brew a batch of decent coffee and make a piece of toast. I remember the loud noise but can't find anything in the house that would explain it. No brooms fallen over or hanging planters shattered on the floor.

Knocking interrupts my search.

I open the front door to a stranger in a plaid shirt and jeans fidgeting on my front porch.

"Morning," he says. "My name's Jake; I live a couple houses over. Could I use your bathroom?" He smiles, apologetic. "I know it's a weird thing to ask, but my plumbing's getting fixed today, and my neighbor isn't answering his door. So, I thought I'd try the next one over." His smile gets desperate. "Please."

"Sure," I say. "It's just through there."

"Thanks so much." He pauses to wipe his shoes on the mat, then runs for the bathroom.

Leaving the front door open, I settle into a kitchen chair with a clear view of the hall. I consider taking out my rifle, just to look intimidating. You never know with the people around here.

A minute later, Jake comes out of the bathroom.

"Thanks again," he says. He turns to leave. Pauses. "What's that?" Jake points at the tuft of white fur on the table.

"Carpet sample," I say.

"Huh. Well, have a good one!" He waves and heads down the three steps to the sidewalk.

I lock the door and watch him through the side window. He turns into the yard two houses over, opens the door, and goes inside. There's a plumber's van parked in front. Seems to support his story. And he was nice, some silver in his grizzled hair. I like that kind of look in men my age.

I shake my head and swipe the werewolf fur from the table. Sending a quick text, I head out to the garage. That's when it clicks. The loud bang from six a.m. The side door to the garage is cracked open, its broken handle hanging from the wood.

Not seeing anyone, I creep into the dim garage and scan for signs of damage. Both of my toolboxes are on the workbench, locks intact. The lawnmower crouches in its usual corner, and the shovels and rakes all seem accounted for. The three-panel fold-down door is secure. Ducking down, I check under the car. Nobody.

That only leaves the car itself. I flip on the overhead light and study the interior through the windshield. I open the back doors to check behind the seats, folding them down to reveal the trunk cavity, but nothing seems out of place.

Could be, it was just someone looking for a place to shoot up or hide from the cops. A quick stop in. Still, I'll need to replace the lock and handle, maybe even the whole door.

I screw a board over the inside of the frame, just enough to keep the door shut while I run my errand.

It's a quick drive to Isabelle's, up the river road and then over a few blocks. She runs a new shop on the strip, sandwiched between a vacant movie theater and a used bookstore.

"I got your text and am very excited!" she exclaims through the fading notes of the door chime. "Hurry up, let me see!"

I meet her at the counter and place the werewolf fur on the glass surface.

Her mouth falls open. "But my darling, it's white! I've never seen such a thing!"

"Their coats change for the winter around here," I explain. "I can assure you, it's the real deal."

"How wonderful!" Isabelle turns to open the cash register. "My customers will be just as intrigued, I'm sure! There must be spells that specifically call for winter fur, of course. I will have to do some research." Isabelle counts out a stack of twenties.

"Business is good?" I ask, catching sight of the fifties in the register.

"Booming! Protection spells are *extremely* popular." She retrieves a wrapped box from under the counter. "I've started making packs so I don't have to measure out the ingredients every time. Would you like to buy one?"

"No thanks."

Isabelle sighs and tucks the box away. "I thought in your line of work, it'd be an easy sell. Ah well." She hands me the stack of bills.

I roll my payout together and stuff in my pocket.

"Do bring me more fur, and even other parts, if you can. It's wonderful doing business with you."

I pick up a new door handle on the way home. As I turn into the driveway, I notice someone standing on my porch.

I roll down my car window, wincing as the cold air seeps in. "Need something?" I yell.

They wave and head over. Plaid shirt, jeans, hiking boots. Jake. "I heard you had some trouble with your garage."

"How?" I ask, suspicious.

"Our mutual neighbour heard a loud noise this morning, saw someone running out of your garage. He called the cops, but no one showed up. So, thought I'd come over and see if I could help."

"They broke the door," I say, suddenly aware of how close he is, the smell of shaving cream and coffee. "I got a new handle, but the jamb's busted."

"You did me a good turn earlier. How about I return the favor?" He smiles, his teeth a little crooked, just off white enough to be naturally attractive.

"Fine." I kick myself for not coming up with a more clever comeback. "I'll park the car out front."

In three hours, he makes a new door, replaces the jamb, and adds an extra lock to keep the door secure.

"Here's some coffee," I announce as I enter the garage.

Jake finishes sweeping up sawdust and bits of wood. The old space heater sputters on the workbench.

"Sorry it's so cold out here."

"I don't mind the cold," he smiles, taking the coffee. There's sawdust in his hair. I want so badly to brush it free.

"How much for the door?" I say instead.

"A favor for a favor," he replies.

"For a neighbor," I rhyme awkwardly.

He's generous with his laughter.

Once he finishes the coffee, he gathers his tools. "I'll see you around," he says.

"Yeah. I'd like that."

A knock on the front door.

"Just a minute!" I yell from the bedroom, applying a final touch of lipstick. Considering myself in the mirror, I wince. It's been a long time since I've been on a date, as the extra layer of make-up and the too-tight sleeveless blouse clearly show. But I have a feeling that Jake won't mind.

We've seen each other on and off the past few weeks. Running into each other on the street, at the grocery store. A follow-up on the garage door, a couple of coffees on the chilly front porch. He's seen me in sweatpants and t-shirts, in jeans and sweaters and coats. I smile a little, wondering if my "first date" look will surprise him.

I take a deep breath .

"Wow," Jake says as soon as I open the door. "Wow, you look incredible!"

"Same to you," I say, taking in the dark turtleneck and dress pants, his silver-shot hair combed back from his broad face. "Very sharp."

"Sorry, I'm a little early."

"It's okay, come in." I wave him inside , his smile throwing a shiver down my spine. Shutting out the cold, I join him on the couch.

"I guess you decided to stick with the hardwood, huh?"

I try to hide my confusion with a nod.

"When I came in to use your bathroom, remember? There was that white fur on the table. You said it was a carpet sample."

"Oh, oh right. Yeah. I thought it would be too hard to keep clean," I stutter, trying to ignore how close his body is to mine.

"You really do look incredible." Jake's hand caresses my bare shoulder. "We have a little bit of time before the dinner reservations."

"Oh?" My senses kick into overdrive as his hand slides to my waist.

"We could," he shifts closer to me, "relax."

His usual smell of shaving cream and coffee is mixed with a rich cologne.

"Relaxing sounds good." I reach over to smooth his hair.

He kisses me, so deeply it aches. His lips move down my neck to my collarbone, kissing, then biting, then—

Biting. Hard. Sinking teeth into skin, deeper, finding blood.

Pushing him off me, I collapse back onto the couch, dizzy. "Jake?" I whimper, pressing a hand to the wound on my chest.

In the middle of the room, Jake straightens, his demeanor completely changed. His eyes are dark flecks in his face. His yellow teeth are bared, stained red.

"I know who you are," he says.

"What...? I'm..."

"I know that you kill werewolves."

"My...job...?"

Jake hunches slightly and shudders. "You killed one nearly a month ago. Do you know who that young woman was?"

I stare at him, warm blood running through my fingers.

"She was my sister," he growls. "One of your neighbors. You didn't even recognize her, did you? When I found out she was dead..."

"I don't know...what you're talking about..."

My denial only angers him more. His hair-backed hands screw into fists, his voice dangerously low. "I broke into your garage. Smelled her blood in your car, saw her fur on your table. I have to put a stop to you. Otherwise, you'll just go on killing us."

Nearly a month ago. The realization steals what little hope I have left. Tomorrow is the last full moon of the year. Already, the effects are starting to show. Jake's teeth are sharper, his silver-streaked hair thicker. His irises are almost completely black.

Stumbling from the couch, I make a run for the gun cabinet. Before I can make it, I'm out cold.

I wake up on the living room floor. Reaching to the pain in my chest, I find something soft. A gauze bandage. The room, drenched in daylight from the windows, is overexposed, too bright. I feel a migraine coming on.

Jake.

Pushing myself up, I run to the door and lock it.

We were supposed to go for dinner. Jake arrived early. On the couch. We were kissing, and he bit me—

He bit me.

I rush to the bedroom and dump my purse on the floor. I scramble to pick my phone out of the mess. My finger hovers over the 9 key. I can't call the police. They'd send an extermination squad if they even suspected—

I tap on my contacts and call Isabelle.

She answers on the second ring. "Annie! This is unexpected! Do you have something else for me?"

"Not right now, Isabelle, uh—hey, I need to know if there's a—a spell? For returning werewolves to humans?"

"A spell? Oh, my darling, no. Otherwise, why would you be in the business of killing them?"

A prickling runs across my bare arms. "Could you do some research, or something? I'll bring you a bunch of fur next time, completely free—"

"I'm sorry, but I can tell you already. There's nothing like that. The poor souls who get turned into werewolves; they're lost."

I throw the phone at the wall.

No way out.

Tonight is the full moon. I catch sight of myself in the mirror. My blouse is crumpled and stained with blood, my make-up smeared, my hair a mess. But underneath, I can spot the signs. Black in the eyes. Sharpening teeth.

I know a werewolf when I see one.

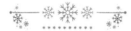

Brittni Brinn writes from a tower and sometimes a cottage in Mi'kma'ki/Nova Scotia. Their stories appear in *At the Lighthouse* (Eibonvale Press), *Your Flight Has Been Cancelled* (Little Ghosts Books), and more! Her weird horror novella, *Misplaced*, is now available through Little Ghosts Books. Read more at brittnibrinn.com.

SNOW ANGEL

ANDY COE

In retrospect, Paul had sensed something was off about his son's behavior from the beginning. He'd just been too absorbed in his work to do anything about it.

"Hi, Daddy!" the boy said cheerily as the back door swung open, letting in a biting gust of winter.

"Close the door behind you, buddy," Paul said, only pulling his eyes away from the glowing screen long enough to see little Dayce clomp into the kitchen on his wet and squeaking boots. His red snowsuit made him look like a miniature Michelin Man.

As he pecked out a few more words on the keyboard, Paul felt a brief pang of guilt. This was one of his rare weekends with Dayce, and he should be outside enjoying the recent snowfall with the little guy. But that could come later. He was so close to finishing this book—a story that had utterly consumed him for the past two weeks—that he would be able to do nothing else until he typed the closing sentence. Besides, Dayce seemed to be doing just fine.

"You coming out soon, Daddy?" Dayce asked. He fumbled for the knob of the patio door with one hand while clutching an assortment of items in the other. sHis smile was wide between his flushed cheeks.

"In a bit, buddy." Paul tried to keep the irritation from his tone, but the boy had broken his train of thought. He flashed another glance at his son, and this time, it lingered long enough for him to notice the items in his arms.

They were some of Dayce's favorite things, and not what you'd take out in the snow: a battered copy of *The Lion, the Witch and the Wardrobe*, which Paul had been reading to him at bedtime; his Nintendo Switch, a pricey bit of electronics that would not fare well if gotten wet; and his dingy stuffed rabbit—the boy's steadfast companion.

"Where are you going with all that?" Paul asked.

Dayce answered as the chill wind again sliced through the open door. "The snow angel wants to see some of my things, so I'm gonna show him."

"Snow angel?" Paul said with an amused smile. The boy was barely five but already had an impressive collection of imaginary friends to call upon; it seemed as though he'd made one more. *Like father, like son,* Paul mused.

Dayce said something else before heading out the door, but Paul didn't catch it. He was already back at the keyboard.

The hard-packed snow crunched beneath his feet with each careful step. And with each of those steps, the temptation to turn and run the other way grew stronger.

He knew he was walking into a trap.

"You are so close, Agent Jansen," whispered the ancient sandpaper voice inside his head. "But what will you do when you find me? You cannot arrest me. You can only serve me. Feed me."

Jansen pushed the voice aside and tried to focus on the trail. Ahead of him, deep trench marks sliced through the snow, streaked with pink and scarlet. Someone had been dragged down this narrow forest path, and they'd been bleeding. Jansen was certain the blood belonged to the missing deputy and that he would not find the man alive.

"Closer, closer..." the sandpaper voice crooned.

Against his better judgment, Jansen's pace quickened. His hands were sweating profusely despite the cold, and the shotgun wavered in his grip. He was approaching a small clearing.

"Closer, closer..."

He crossed the threshold.

Jansen had witnessed many horrors throughout his career, but what he saw still shook him. Towering over him, its skeletal branches stretching across the length of the clearing, was a massive, ancient oak tree. At the base of the tree was a hollow, and inside the dark, yawning mouth of this hollow was what he feared were the remains of Deputy Blake.

A hand.

An ear.

A scattering of red teeth.

The gore-stained snow spilled out of the mouth of the hollow as if the tree had devoured the deputy and purged what little it could not digest.

"Tell me, Agent Jansen," the voice whispered from the hollow, from his head. "What will you give me to avoid the same fate?"

In answer, Jansen steadied the barrel of the shotgun at the mouth of the hollow...

The story had come to him in a series of dreams.

They were the most intense and vivid dreams he'd ever experienced. Horribly fantastic interpretations of a series of real-life disappearances. Decades ago, in the large expanse of woods bordering Paul's backyard, eleven people had gone missing over a five-year period. No clue as to their fates had ever been discovered, and the disappearances were a local mystery to this day. Paul's dreams suggested it had been the work of a demon named Abaddon. It hid within its dark hollow, tempting its prey with false promises. Luring them in, then pulling them into that black mouth to hell before they realized the deception. Never to be seen again.

It was dark stuff, to be sure, but it had cured his writer's block, and that was something bestselling author Paul Watts was not going to take for granted. So, he'd impulse-bought the house where he now worked and let his close proximity to the local legend fuel his creativity. He'd cranked out three hundred pages in just under two weeks, but now things were starting to sputter a little toward the end. He hated to admit it, but Dayce was getting in the way.

Why, when he was getting so close to the end, did it have to be his weekend with the little guy?

As if Paul's guilty thoughts had summoned him, the back patio door again flew open, and Dayce clomped in. This time the boy said nothing, only marched into the kitchen with a skip in his step and opened the refrigerator.

Guess it is about lunchtime, Paul thought. *Better make the little guy something before he makes too big a mess.* But there was a dangling, incomplete sentence on the screen before him, beckoning him to finish it. So Paul finished it. And the next one. And the next. A few minutes later, he only spared the boy the briefest glance as Dayce headed back outside, his little arms brimming with Tupperware containers of leftovers.

For his snow angel, Paul figured.

Dayce stepped carefully on his trek back to the old tree, trying his best to place his feet in the holes in the deep snow his boots had already made along the path. Despite his best efforts, he still occasionally stamped a new print, causing him to stumble and nearly drop his load.

It didn't help that he was also distracted; he couldn't stop thinking about how he was doing something he wasn't supposed to. If Daddy knew he was playing in the woods, he'd be very angry. The woods were off limits.

But maybe Daddy *did* know, Dayce thought. After all, he could clearly see out the back door from where he did his writing; Daddy probably watched him walk into the woods the very first time the snow angel called to him.

As Dayce entered the clearing, one more justification came to him: he wasn't even that far from the house. If Daddy knew where to look, he could probably see him through the trees from his office. With his arms still full of Tupperware containers, Dayce looked back at the house to try to verify his assumption.

"Have you forgotten about me, little one?" the snow angel asked. The whispered words inside his head startled him, and Dayce dropped the three containers into the snow.

"I'm sorry," he said, kneeling to amend his mistake.

"Don't be sorry. Simply feed me, as you promised."

Dayce grabbed a Tupperware container, brushed the snow from it, and stood to face the tree. It was a very old oak tree with a wide trunk that was hollow at the base; Dayce thought the hollow would be big enough for him to stand inside, were it not mostly filled with a drift of snow. Beneath that drift was the snow angel.

He pried the lid from the container and released the smell of rubbery, day-old chicken nuggets into the cold air. He clumsily fished one out with a red mitten and tossed it into the drift that spilled from the tree hollow. It sat there for a moment among the other artifacts he'd left for his new friend—his Nintendo Switch; the paperback copy of *The Lion, the Witch and the Wardrobe*; and Jack, his bunny rabbit—then was sucked into the drift, as if pulled down from below.

Dayce tossed the other four nuggets in after the first. As each one disappeared into the snow, he jumped a little out of excitement and fear. While he very much enjoyed his new friend's company, there was also something scary about the angel. Like how he could only hear it inside his head. Or how that soothing whisper also worried him. It made him wonder if the snow angel was really his friend.

"I have enjoyed your gifts," the snow angel said, *"but I am still very hungry. What else did you bring me?"*

Without hesitation, Dayce grabbed the largest container and pulled off the lid. His nose wrinkled at the smell as he looked down at Daddy's uneaten dinner from the night before: a thick-cut pork chop glazed in gooey garlic sauce. Like the nuggets, Dayce fumbled it into his red mitten and prepared to fling it.

"That is far too large for me to eat in one bite, little one," the snow angel crooned. *"You will need to cut it up. Did you bring the knife?"*

Dayce had grabbed the knife from the butcher block at the snow angel's request but had been hoping he wouldn't have to use it. He wasn't very good at cutting up food. Still, he removed his mittens and gently pulled the small steak knife from the pocket of his snowsuit. The stainless steel handle was very cold.

"Please," the snow angel urged companionably. *"Cut it into smaller bites for me."*

Dayce sat down in the snow and placed the slab of pork chop back in its container. Brow furrowed in concentration, he began gently working at the meat with the knife. The garlic sauce caused it to slip around in the container, evading his blade, so—against his better judgment—Dayce gripped the edges of the pork chop with one little hand and sawed diligently with the other.

It was easier than he would have thought. The knife was small but sharp, and after just a few strokes back and forth, he was—

"Hurry, boy," the snow angel demanded. It was not a whisper inside Dayce's head but a shout that scared him and caused his knife hand to slip. Dayce saw the blood before he felt the cut.

It welled up on the tip of his finger like a crimson tear, then began to drip steadily into the plastic container, mixing with the garlic sauce. A storm of emotions swept over Dayce: worry over his finger; shame at being startled; and guilt from disobeying Daddy.

He began to cry.

"Fear not, little one," the snow angel whispered. *"Give me your finger, and I will make it whole again."*

Dayce wanted to let his new friend help, but he was also becoming afraid of the angel beneath the snow. There was something in its voice that hadn't been there before. Something that felt wrong.

"Give me your finger, boy." Not a request, but a demand.

Dayce scrambled to his feet and turned to run back home. But the snow angel found the words that changed his mind.

"You are afraid of me," it stated plainly. *"But I think you are more afraid of your father. Think of the trouble you'll be in when Daddy sees what you've been up to. When he learns you've been playing out in the forbidden woods and hurt yourself doing it."*

The snow angel was right. If he ran straight home, he would have to admit everything to Daddy, and Daddy would have to stop his writing to fix him up. He would be very angry.

"But he doesn't have to know," the snow angel whispered as if reading his thoughts. *"Let me fix you."*

There was still an inexplicable malice in the voice, but Dayce still turned to it. His boots crunched in the snow as he approached the base of the hollow. A spotty trail of blood from his finger followed in his wake and turned the snow pink. When he was as close as he would allow himself to get, Dayce extended his shaking finger over the drift of snow inside the hollow.

The hand that emerged from the drift was gnarled and skeletal, an extension of the tree itself. The bony fingers were curled into a tight fist, and they slowly unfurled like a blooming flower.

Dayce placed his bleeding finger inside the open palm.

THE END.

Paul leaned back in his chair, hands laced behind his head, and stared at the words. A mere twelve days had passed between his opening sentence and those capstone letters—a fraction of the time spent on his previous works. Paul attributed it to the vivid dreams he'd had since moving into the house. Dreams that demanded he spin them into a story and put it all to page.

But now he had come to the end of the demon Abaddon's story. After the breakneck speed in which it had been written, Paul was content to simply sit back and give himself to the familiar mix of pride and loss that always visited him upon a story's completion.

For Paul, his stories were his children. Conceived in a burst of imagination and nurtured through the written word, they eventually matured enough to live outside of him. His pride came from watching those paper children enter the hands of eager readers across the world, and the loss stemmed from the void every parent is left with when their children finally leave home.

Children. Leaving home.

Paul snapped his head to the side to look down the short stretch of hallway connecting his office with the kitchen. The door that led out onto the back patio was clearly in view. When he realized that the glare of the sun beaming through the door's glass panes had been replaced by the dull murk of approaching twilight, panic set in. He hadn't seen or heard Dayce come through that door in a very long time.

Panic turned to terror as he ran from room to room, shouting his son's name, threatening big trouble if he didn't show himself *right this minute.* His frantic search eventually returned full circle to the back patio door.

When he opened the door and saw the line of small boot prints leading from the patio into the dark woods, Paul let his terror fully consume him.

It didn't register for Paul that he'd been running through the snow in his bare feet until he stubbed his toe and fell to his knees. But by that time, the burning cold biting at his exposed flesh was a distant concern. He was too lost within the strange confluence of worlds that had enveloped him. With every frantic step, it became harder and harder to separate reality from fiction.

Was he following the little guy's boot prints or ragged, bloody trenches in the snow?

Was he alone in these woods, or was there a voice somewhere nearby *(in his mind)* urging him onward?

Would he find his son at the end of this snowy trail or a monster?

Paul stopped briefly to marshal both his stamina and his sanity.

This line of thinking was absurd; he needed to get his head on straight. These woods were home to eleven unexplained disappearances, but the key word was *unexplained.* No bodies had ever been found or any other scraps of evidence hinting at foul play. Only local legend and Paul's own twisted imagination had given birth to the horrors that now tugged at his mind, nothing more. He was not following in Agent Jansen's footsteps.

There were no bloody trench marks in the snow. And there certainly wasn't a voice—

"Closer..."

Paul tried to breathe, but his fear did not let him. Everything seemed to go silent—the faint breeze through the trees, his heartbeat—leaving only the voice.

"Closer, Paul...closer..."

He was succumbing to the stress of losing Dayce, Paul reasoned. His terror had crested to a point where he was beginning to hallucinate. *Just keep following the boot prints and ignore everything else,* he told himself. *You'll find the little guy at the end, and you can both go home. Maybe have a nice hot cup of cocoa afterward, and*

(delete that fucking book you wrote)

"Just a bit closer, Paul. After all this time, I'm so very anxious to meet you."

Follow the boot prints. Ignore everything else.

Paul repeated this like a mantra as he urged his frozen feet forward. He'd never changed out of his pajamas this morning, and now the cold was burrowed deep inside him like a parasite, leeching his vitality. His teeth chattered.

"Follow...the boot prints...ignore...everything else..."

"That's it. Almost there, Paul."

Paul's mantra died on his lips when he saw the snow-packed trail widen ahead of him. It was opening into a clearing, and he feared what he would find there.

But fear was all it was, he told himself as he pressed onward. Special Agent Ben Jansen was not real. The dismembered remains of Deputy

Blake were not real. The demon Abaddon was not real. Paul clutched at these truths as he walked into the clearing.

Walked into his dreams.

The old, towering oak tree was here, though the bony fingers of its branches did not veil the dusking sky as in his story. Nor was the dark mouth of the tree's hollow stuffed with gore—only a drift of snow.

And Dayce's things.

They sat in the snow, spaced evenly in a semicircle around the mouth of the hollow, like items offered in tribute. A trio of Tupperware containers Paul recognized from his fridge were also there; all were open and empty. In the thin glaze of garlic that remained at the bottom of one container, Paul saw streaks of red that made his stomach lurch.

Dayce was nowhere to be seen.

"Finally, after all this time, we meet." The voice was thin and raspy, like sandpaper. It was in Paul's head. *"What will you do, Paul?"*

Paul wasn't sure what he was going to do but could think of several things he wished he *had* done. He wished he'd kept a better eye on Dayce throughout the day. He wished he'd resisted the lure of his dreams. He wished he'd never written that goddamn book. Instead of saying any of that, however, he said:

"I'm going to get my son back."

"Is that so?" said the voice. *"Will you be the hero of this story, Paul? I must admit, you will need to do much more than peck a few fancy words on your keyboard to banish the* real *me. This is not a dream."*

No, this was not a dream; as impossible as it seemed, Paul knew that much. The demon Abaddon was real, and he stood in its presence.

Paul was no warrior, no Agent Jansen; there was nothing he could do to fight this thing, but he had to try something. For Dayce's sake.

He made an offer.

"Give me my son, and I'll give you anything you want in return."

"Anything I want?"

"Anything."

"What if I want you, *Paul?"*

"If you'll return my boy," Paul said through his chattering teeth, "then you can have me."

"Very well," Abaddon said as a swift gust of snow swirled around Paul's bare ankles. *"Give me what I require, and you shall see your son again."*

Paul looked down and saw the knife.

It emerged handle-first from the snow between his numb and frozen feet like a hell-spawned Excalibur. As he gripped it with trembling fingers, it occurred to him that, like the Tupperware, this blade came from his kitchen. It made him sick to think that he'd unwittingly let the little guy walk out of the house with it.

Give me what I require.

Paul knew what that was. The eleven fictional victims in his story had offered the same.

He brought the steak knife to his wrist and ran it gently across the delicate skin. Blood ran red and hot into the snow.

"Good, good...closer...closer..."

Paul extended his weeping wrist into the hollow. His head was already swimming, but he held tight to the knife. When the demon emerged, he would plunge the blade into its black heart before it could register his betrayal.

But his strike never came. The knife dropped from his limp fingers the moment the snow gave up its secret.

The arm that emerged was sleeved in a red nylon coat. The small, cherubic fingers were curled into a tight fist, and they slowly unfurled like a blooming flower.

Andy Coe lives in northern Colorado with his spoiled cat, Queenie. By day he is a software engineer, but by night he spends his hours writing horror. He has published both short- and long-form fiction on Kindle Vella and is currently writing a full-length novel entitled The Devil's Keepsake.

Also From Undertaker Books

Ink Vine

Elizabeth Broadbent

Shadows of Appalachia

D.L. Winchester

The Taste of Women

Cyan LeBlanc

Mastering The Art of Female Cookery

Cyan LeBlanc

In Memory of Exoskeltons

Rebecca Cuthbert

Stories To Take To Your Grave: Vol. 1(Anthology)

A Terrible Place and Other Flashes of Darkness

D.L. Winchester

The Triangle + The Deep Double Feature

Robert P. Ottone

Silent Mine

C.M. Saunders

Odd Jobs: Six Files from the Department of Inhuman Resources(Anthology)

Judicial Homicide (Anthology)

Bodily Harm

Deborah Sheldon

The Screaming House

D.L. Winchester

Wilder Creatures

Nadia Steven Rysing

Ninety-Eight Sabers

Elizabeth Broadbent

Self-Made Monsters

Rebecca Cuthbert

Made in United States
Cleveland, OH
23 December 2024

12532154R00095